To. Markus,

The Grand Adventures of
Ribbit the Frog

Book One
Lily Pad Hollow in Trouble

By Kylie O'Brien Hall

Dream Big!

Kylie O'Brien Hall

For my son, Ryland – you are my greatest adventure.

The Great Defender of Lily Pad Hollow

"Take that!" Ribbit cried out as he lunged toward the enemy, his mighty sword glistening in the sunlight like the scales of a fish. "Your number is up, Megalith. Prepare to die, you rotten mongoose!"

Without a second to lose, Megalith darted out of the way of Ribbit's sword, splashing into the muddy shallows of the pond. He stood up and shook the mud off of his thick, spiky fur before he turned to face the brave young frog. His feverish, unblinking eyes locked with Ribbit's and his back arched, ready to mount his attack. As quick as the wind, the mongoose launched himself toward Ribbit with his mouth wide open, baring his dagger-sharp teeth. Ribbit could feel the breeze of his attacker against his skin as he leapt high into the air, narrowly missing his enemy's advances and landing gracefully on a giant boulder beside the water's edge. That was a close one.

The treacherous battle wore on as Ribbit tried desperately to ward off Megalith's deadly strikes, hopping to and fro, his sword slicing recklessly through the air. He had to win this battle; he just had to! The fate of Lily Pad Hollow depended on it. Megalith was bent on devouring the frogs of the Hollow and Ribbit was not going to let that happen; not to the frogs of his town.

After a couple near misses and a few successful jabs, Ribbit finally had the evildoer right where he wanted him—cornered against the giant boulder. Ribbit held his mighty sword up to Megalith's neck, as the mongoose's eyes grew wide with terror. There was nowhere to run. He would not escape this time.

"Prepare to meet your doom, Megalith. I warned you that it would get to this. No one messes with my town. This is for the Hollow!" Ribbit bellowed as he raised his sword for the final blow. This would be the end of that pesky mongoose once and for . . .

"Ha! Ha! Ha!" a voice snickered, but it wasn't coming from the mongoose. No, it was coming from someplace else; like it was far away in some other world. "Look at the dork!" It echoed in his ear.

Suddenly, Ribbit was jolted back into reality, his once mighty sword now revealed for the pathetic cattail it was. His enemy disappeared back into the world of imagination, to be defeated another day, and there he stood: a young, scrawny frog looking more pathetic than ever—exposed for what he really was.

"What are you doing, loser?" another voice snarled. It was so cold and cruel that it could be none other than Squiggy, Dragonfly Elementary's meanest bully. And where there was Squiggy, Kilroy wasn't far behind.

"Uh, nothing," Ribbit mumbled to his feet, letting his "mighty sword" fall to the ground. He often played out his imaginary battles, but never in front of the other frogs at school; especially not Squiggy and Kilroy. He wasn't a little tadpole anymore, but he still reveled in how it felt to pretend to be someone else, if only for a little while.

"Oh, no! I think it was *something*, don't you Kilroy?" Squiggy shot Ribbit a look, like a predator honing in on his prey, as he walked over and scooped the cattail that lay at Ribbit's feet.

"Yeah, it was definitely something. Who's Megalith anyway? Another loser friend of yours?" Kilroy's eyes darted about as he pretended to look for another animal, though he knew very well that Ribbit was alone.

"I don't know what you're talking about," Ribbit shuddered. Why was it that he could stand up to the most evil villains in his imagination, but he couldn't say a word to these goons? And now Squiggy was holding his favorite sword. More than anything, he wanted to rush at Squiggy and snatch the cattail back, but his fear anchored him in place. This was not going to end well.

"Oh, I know who he is, Kilroy! It's so obvious." Squiggy smacked his hand on his forehead as if he had just been enlightened. "Megalith is Ribbit's best friend. And you know why he's his best friend?" He elbowed Kilroy in the ribs, a look of sinister delight on his face, as he gently used the cattail to caress under his chin.

"Because he's a loser like Ribbit?" Kilroy chortled. Ribbit clenched his fists as if he wanted to wipe that smirk off Kilroy's face.

"No, although I'm sure he is, no doubt," he snickered, his narrow eyes full of hate. "He's Ribbit's best friend because he's INVISIBLE! No one in their right mind would want to be seen with a loser like that!" They both let out a roar of scorned laughter, and then Squiggy held out Ribbit's cattail sword in both hands, as if he were presenting it. Instead, he snapped it in half, breaking Ribbit's heart along with it.

Not my favorite cattail! Ribbit's inner voice screamed. *It took me weeks to find one that would stand up straight!* He jolted forward to pick up the remains of his fallen friend and his hands trembled as he held the pieces in his hand.

"Aw, did I bweak the poor tadpole's wittle weapon?" Squiggy teased with an unnatural smile. Ribbit didn't respond, but simply stared at his broken sword, trying not to cry. No matter what he did, he couldn't cry.

"C'mon. Let's get out of here. We don't want to be seen with this loser. Later, dorkface!" The two frogs chuckled as they turned to leave. "Oh and thanks for handling Megalith. I don't know what we would do without you." They both burst out in hysterics, grasping at their stomachs as they walked out of sight.

—

Ribbit could have kicked himself. His life was officially over. It was only a matter of time before Squiggy and Kilroy told all the frogs at school about what had happened and no one would look at him the same way again. Why did he just stand there and let them treat him that way? Why didn't he stick up for himself? Surely, if Croak were there he would have knocked those bullies over for saying such cruel things. And Phinn would have at least had some sassy remark or comeback, like "it takes one to know one" or something like that. But no, not Ribbit. Instead, he just stood there completely motionless, letting his heart be crushed into a million little pieces without uttering a single word of protest. Why couldn't real life be more like his imaginary world?

A Little Frog with a Big Dream

Whiz, a pink tongue flew through the air.

Whoosh, another struck quickly at the fly zipping by, narrowly missing it.

Snap, and the fly was gone.

The crowd burst into a cheer; Speckles, the "underfrog" and the only girl in the entire fly-eating competition had won.

High above the small town, a banner the color of daffodils waved gracefully in the wind, with the words "Lily Pad Hollow's Annual Fly-Eating Contest" written in a shiny apple red. Beneath it, Main Street was teeming with frogs of every age and every color, gathering to witness the fly eating in all of its glory. Young frogs sat in the front, cross-legged, excitement painted on their shiny, round faces as they clapped frantically for the unexpected winner. Older frogs relaxed under colorful umbrellas that lined the street, chatting among themselves and drinking fly lattes while keeping an eye on their little ones. When the excitement was over, all the frogs joined in a celebratory picnic and barbeque to eat grilled water strider burgers and discuss the goings on in their everyday lives; all the frogs, that is, except for three.

*****

Ribbit, Phinn, and Croak sat on the bank, dipping their webbed toes into the cool water and sipping blended mosquito milkshakes, a daily part of their summer routine.

"I just didn't see that coming . . ." Phinn remarked with disbelief on his face as he took off his glasses and gently wiped them with his shorts pocket. "Speckles came out of nowhere. Who knew that girl could put away ten flies in one sitting?"

"I couldn't believe it! I mean, I knew that girl could eat, but geez!" Ribbit giggled.

"She didn't out-eat Gilly from last year's competition, though. Remember, he ate fifteen flies in one minute," Croak pointed out.

"True," Phinn nodded. "But they also had more flies in the competition last year than they had this year. Why do you think they only had twenty-five to start with? They've always had a standard forty fly entry for the competition ever since we were tadpoles," Phinn asked, chewing on the straw of his mosquito milkshake and tilting his head in thought.

"I don't know. I heard a rumor that they couldn't catch as many as they did last year. And come to think of it, I haven't seen as many flies around here like there usually are," Ribbit said. As the words left his mouth he suddenly wondered if he should be worried.

"You're right," Phinn said, his eyes squinted in thought. "I haven't seen a swarm of flies come around here in quite a while. Seems like we only get a few stragglers here and there."

Ribbit put down his milkshake and furrowed his brow as he looked out upon the cattails that surrounded their small town. *What's going on out there?* he wondered, his imagination aflutter with the possibilities of what lay just beyond their borders. Since no frog had ever dared to leave (and lived to tell about it), there really was no way to be sure.

"Well, it doesn't really matter how many flies were entered in the contest," Croak said, quickly changing the subject. "Speckles still out-ate me. I don't think I could eat that many flies in one sitting." He looked down and rubbed his big round belly. Leave it to Croak to lighten the mood and make their worries disappear.

"Wow, I think that's the first time I've ever heard you say that, Croak," Ribbit teased, flashing Croak a mischievous grin. He was no longer consumed with worrisome thoughts, not when he had better things to do, like giving Croak a hard time.

"Very funny, Mr. Comedian," Croak said as he knocked Ribbit over with a jerk from his husky shoulder, launching him face first into the muddy shallows. He and Phinn had a good laugh, as Ribbit hopped frantically trying to wipe off the scum.

"Get it off me! Get it off me!" Ribbit cried, leaping high into the air and flailing his arms like a crazed frog.

This set Croak and Phinn into an even bigger laughing fit, both of them rolling on the ground, holding their stomachs, tears welling in their eyes, as they looked at a filthy, mud-spattered Ribbit. It was only after their laughing subsided that Phinn grabbed a hollowed-out acorn shell, filled it with clean pond water, and splashed Ribbit. The brown muck slowly dripped down his body, revealing the smooth green skin that lay underneath, like hot fudge over a grasshopper sundae.

"Nice, Croak. Thanks for the dirt bath," Ribbit muttered, using a small leaf in an attempt to clean the gunk out of his ears.

"Didn't think I bumped you that hard, buddy. Guess I don't know my own strength," Croak chuckled, gently patting Ribbit on the back. Ribbit couldn't help but smile at how ridiculous he had probably just looked, all covered in mud, screaming like a little tadpole. He wanted to be mad at Croak for knocking him into the sludge, but he just couldn't bring himself to be upset. Phinn and Croak were the only frogs in the Hollow who stood by him when others mocked him and understood him in ways only the best of friends could. Their friendship meant more to him than anything.

Just then, the warm summer breeze blew through Lily Pad Hollow, as it often did this time of year, causing the cattails surrounding the borders of the town to sway as if dancing to a summer tune.

"Hey guys, you ever wonder what life is like outside of Lily Pad Hollow?" Ribbit asked. He was obsessed with the mysteries that lay just beyond their boundaries. Were there other places like Lily

—

13

Pad Hollow out there in the world? Were there different animals, other than the usual pond critters that inhabited his town? Questions sparked in Ribbit's mind like fireflies on a clear summer night; questions that no frog in Lily Pad Hollow could answer.

"No," Croak blurted without even the slightest bit of interest. He continued to pick up small stones and throw them into the pond, as he was doing before.

Phinn adjusted his glasses. "I've thought about what it might be like outside the boundaries, but none of those thoughts have been good ones." He looked uneasily at the swaying cattails, a shiver overtaking his body. "I heard that six summers ago some frog dared to go beyond our borders. The idiot actually went strutting through the cattails thinking he was going to be a hero or something. Any-way, they say that they heard the most terrifying noise come from the other side and that was the last they ever heard from him."

"Oh, that's just a story the old frogs made up to keep us here. That never really happened," Ribbit said doubtfully, although he looked a little more curiously at the cattails. It was as if they were waving at him, beckoning him to pass through their boundaries and explore the unknown.

Phinn spun his head toward Ribbit so quickly his mosquito milkshake sloshed over his cup and dripped into the water like a tiny brown explosion on the pond's calm surface. "Oh, yes it did! My cousin's friend's brother saw the whole thing," he snapped, his feet no longer whisking the water playfully. "Well, if your cousin's friend's brother saw it, then it must be true." Ribbit said as he rolled his eyes. "Should I also check under my bed every night for monsters? What does your cousin's friend's brother think of those?"

Croak couldn't help but chuckle as he continued throwing stones, stashing a few keepers in the pockets of the raggedy vest he always wore.

"Fine. Don't believe me," Phinn said in a shrill tone. "But I know it's true. That's why I'm never even going close to those things." He began licking the sticky milkshake off his hand and the side of his cup with his long pink tongue, believing the conversation was over.

Ribbit scooted closer to Phinn, gently putting his arm around his friend. "Never? Not even if you found out there was a whole village of frogs just like you beyond the borders? Frogs who would rather spend their time looking at different plants and examining the world around them than swimming or leaping? Frogs who admire green spotted faces? You're not at all interested?" He asked, raising his brows mischievously.

Phinn's round, bulging eyes lit up as he wiggled out of Ribbit's arm and began pointing and waving a sharp finger in disapproval. "Oh, no! I know what you're up to! Don't even think about it, Ribbit!" He wrinkled his nose as if he would never allow such a thing to happen. "Every frog knows that there's no better and safer place to be than Lily Pad Hollow. You would have to be totally brain-dead to even think of pulling a stunt like that."

Ribbit flashed a playful grin and gently elbowed Phinn on his thin twiggy arm. "Oh, come on, Phinny boy! There's a whole world out there for exploring," he said, waving his hand gracefully. "You mean to tell me that you would be totally happy living here, doing the same boring thing over and over again, every day for the rest of your life?"

Ribbit was hoping that his friends would see that living confined in one place for your whole life was a crazy idea. He had long, toned legs that were made for exploration. He had a sharp, witty mind that was made for discovery. He had a heart that longed for adventure. He had all of these things, yet there was still one thing that he needed for his great journeys: companions. He knew he could talk Croak into accompanying him, but Phinn was a different story. He was logical and, well, a "scaredy frog," so convincing him to take such a dangerous risk would be no easy task.

Phinn pushed his glasses higher on his nose, lifted his head high and said confidently, "Absolutely! I hope to stay in Lily Pad Hollow until the day I die. I want to be like Old Frog Amphibilus, rocking in my old chair, drinking Flytinis and listening to the sweet sounds of banjos until the time comes for me to go to that great lily pad up in the sky." As Phinn went into detail about his life as an old frog, Ribbit could see the gleam in his eye. He really meant it! He, along with all of the other frogs in Lily Pad Hollow, was completely content with a simple life behind the confines of the cattail borders. This was just something that Ribbit could not understand.

"What about you, Croak? You really want to stay in this muddy prison like Mr. Boring over here?" Ribbit asked, pointing his thumb toward a glaring Phinn.

"Umm . . . I guess I never really thought about it before," Croak said. He squinted thoughtfully at the cattails for a moment. His mouth crinkled to the side like he had just sucked on a ripe lemon. "I guess it would be pretty cool to see what's out there," he shrugged. Phinn shot him a look so venomous that he quickly chang-ed his response. "Umm . . . I mean . . . I'm cool here. Who needs the outside world anyway?" His eyes made their way back to the pond as he picked up his stones and continued throwing.

Phinn's face relaxed into a satisfied smile as he slurped up the last few drops of his mosquito milkshake.

Ribbit wasn't giving up so easily. "Well, you guys may want to stay here in boring Lily Pad Hollow, but not me! I'm gonna see the world!" Ribbit exclaimed, poking his thumb in his puffed-out chest. "I'm gonna go on grand adventures and I'm gonna fight off bad guys and find hidden treasures." He grabbed a stick from the shallows and began to flail it in the air as his mighty sword. "I'm gonna duel with thieves and battle fierce predators."

He acted out this valiant scene with his stick in hand, slicing the air and stabbing his imaginary foes, before standing victoriously and breathlessly on a rock beside the pond's edge. Once he had his breath back, he raised his "sword" and continued. "Then, I'm gonna come back to Lily Pad Hollow a hero and everyone is going to cheer and cry out, 'Ribbit is the bravest frog to ever live!'" His heart began to race just thinking about his grand adventure and a parade of grasshoppers hopped deliriously in his stomach. He took a deep bre-ath to keep the commotion in his body at bay and continued his speech. "And I will never be forgotten because I will have done something truly special." He paused for dramatic effect, looked his friends straight in the eyes, pointed his finger at them and said in a low, raspy voice, "I, my friends, will have lived!"

Just saying the words made him feel victorious and drowsy with delight. It was his destiny to go out into the world and it was the destiny of his friends to join him on his great journey. And how could they not? After a speech like that, they had to feel the same grasshoppers in the pit of their stomachs and they had to feel compelled to get out in the world and do something great. He was certain they would look him square in the eyes, grab his hand, and pledge their allegiance to his cause. He was wrong.

After a moment of stunned silence, Croak and Phinn glanced at each other, and then burst out laughing.

Ribbit held his head up high, brushed the dried mud off of his shorts, and faced his hysterical friends. "Fine. You guys can laugh all you want. But you'll see. One day, my adventures will be legendary." And with that, he hopped home, more determined than ever to become the hero he had always dreamed of being. He would show them what a brave and mighty frog he really was.

A Log We Call Home

Darkness began to streak its inky fingers across the sky as Ribbit walked up the path to the old hollowed out log by the edge of the pond that he called home. Although it wasn't even close to being the biggest house in the Hollow, it was cozy and had the warm comfort only a home can bring.

As he walked through the door, he was met by the savory smell of his mother's fly stew. The delicious aroma gave him a warm feeling in the pit of his stomach. His mother made the best fly stew in all of Lily Pad Hollow and nobody enjoyed it more than he did.

"Ribbit!" Zippy cried, running happily to the door to greet her brother. All Ribbit could see was a blur of her lime green head that was speckled with tiny polka dots. It was almost as if someone had taken a paintbrush and lovingly shaken it over her entire body, just to make her different.

"Hey there, Ribbykins! How was your day?" His mother's voice rang out from the kitchen.

Yes, she called him Ribbykins and if anyone else had called him that name, he would have hated it. But, since it was his mom, he put up with it and secretly enjoyed being her little Ribbykins.

"Hi, Ma," he replied, as he set down his pack and entered the kitchen, Zippy close at his side, examining his every move. He gave his mother a kiss on her cheek as she furiously stirred the big, bubbling pot of fly stew. "My day was okay. Just went down to the pond, threw some rocks, and hung out with the guys and stuff."

"Ha, ha! You look messy, Ribbit!" Zippy giggled, pointing a small speckled finger at his dirty shorts.

His mother stopped her stirring long enough to look him up and down, her brow furrowed in confusion. "What on earth happened to you? You look like you are caked in mud! It wasn't those Squiggy and Kilroy boys again, was it? Because if they did something to you, their mothers are going to hear about it!"

Being so caught up the excitement of imagining his great voyage, Ribbit had forgotten about the little dirt bath Croak had given him. He could only imagine what he must look like. "No, Ma, it's nothing like that. I was just fooling around with the guys. No big deal. Is Dad around?"

His mother muttered something about "boys being boys" as she took out a small spoon and tasted her fly stew, something she always did just before serving it to make sure that it was just right.

"Mmm . . ." she mumbled under her breath, closing her eyes and taking a moment to let the flavor kick in. "Maybe just a pinch more." Then she opened her eyes, as if coming out of a stew trance and remembered that her son had just asked her a question. "Oh, sorry my darling little tadpole. Just trying to make sure that this fly stew has enough moss in it." She reached high up in the cupboards and grabbed a small jar labeled, "Pond Moss."

"Let me do it! Let me do it!" Zippy cried, grabbing the pond moss and putting a few long strands into the bubbling creation.

His mother smiled at her little helper, then turned back to him. "Your father is around back right now fixing the hole that darn termite created. Would you be a dear and tell him that supper is ready?" Then she reached for four bowls and began filling them with her savory stew while humming a sweet melody that she had sung ever since Ribbit was a little egg.

Ribbit knew that when his mother asked him to "be a dear," it was her nice way of telling him to do something and he really had no choice in the matter. So he swiftly went around back to find his father, following the familiar banging of his father's stone hammer. Although his father wasn't much of a carpenter, he was always tinkering with things.

"Heya, Dad!" Ribbit croaked as he approached.

His father looked up as he crouched by a small hole that wasn't anywhere near being fixed yet. In fact, it appeared as if he might have done more damage trying to fix the problem, but at least he'd tried.

"Hey, kiddo! How's it going?"

"I'm good. Just got home from hanging with the guys." Ribbit crouched down beside him, picked up another stone hammer, and tried to do what he could to help.

"Oh, yeah? So, how's the future of Lily Pad Hollow looking? Did you guys fight off all the bad guys and find the treasure?" his father asked, wiping the sweat from his brow.

"You betchya," Ribbit smiled. Nobody quite understood him the way his father did.

"That's what I like to hear. So, let me guess. Your mother sent you out here because supper's ready, huh?"

"Yeah, and it smells really good. Why don't you call it a night, Dad, and I'll have Phinn and Croak over tomorrow to help us fix that hole?" Ribbit knew that the three of them together had a much better chance of fixing that hole than his father had working alone.

His father gave him a wink and wiped his brow again with his arm. "You're a good boy," he said. "Now, let's go get us some grub." Then he slung his arm around his son and left his project to be finished another day.

Supper was just as delicious as Ribbit had anticipated, and he ate every bite, licking the bowl clean. It was his job to help his father clear the table and do the dishes, as his mother and Zippy prepared hot reed grass tea. Once the dishes were all scrubbed, dried, and put away, Ribbit put on his pajamas, helped Zippy get into her pajamas, and then joined his parents in the living room. Every night, his family would sit in the living room and drink warm tea while sitting beside the roaring fire and reading a bedtime story. He loved getting all snuggled up with his parents and reading fascinating stories together. Mostly they read stories by Ribbit's favorite author, R.T. Hopkins. Ribbit couldn't get enough of his books. One of his favorites was about a little frog who was snatched up by humans, but managed to escape, leading into a whirlwind adven-ture. This brave little frog had to fight off terrifying humans and their monster pets with their giant paws and straw-like whiskers. He loved to read stories about humans. And even though no frog in Lily Pad Hollow had ever seen a human and most believed them to be mythical creatures, he secretly believed that they were real (though he would never admit it to anyone—after all, he wasn't a little tadpole anymore).

After the story was finished, Ribbit's parents tucked Zippy into bed first, then took him to his room and tucked him into bed. Every night they would kiss him on the forehead, uncover his firefly nightlight jar, and would tell him they loved him, each time in a different way.

The night before, his mother had said, "I love you more than there are clouds in the sky." His father had said, "I love you more th-an there are speckles on Zippy." Ribbit always looked forward to this little game because it kept him guessing how his parents would measure their love for him each night.

Tonight, his mother kissed him gently on the forehead and said, "Ribbit, I love you more . . ." She paused to think a second.

". . . more than there are minnows in the pond." He smiled because he knew that there were plenty of minnows in the pond. Then his father leaned in and kissed him on the forehead and said, "Son, I love you more than . . ." He also paused, thinking. ". . . more than . . ." he stammered. "Hold on, I'll get this," he said, scrunching his face to the side, deep in thought. Suddenly, his face lit up with an idea. "Ribbit, I love you more than you love flies." His father tickled his tummy and they both burst out laughing. He'd never felt more loved in his life than when his parents tucked him into bed.

"Okay, you two. It's time for sleep," his mother said, her voice as smooth as silk. "Sweet dreams, my little Ribbykins." His parents slowly crept out of the room, shutting the door, but leaving a little crack so he could hear them moving about the house.

He closed his eyes as visions of noble conquests played out in his mind, and he fell asleep to the faint sound of banjos and crickets.

Trouble in Lily Pad Hollow

The following week, Ribbit sat out on his front yard playing with his pet snail, Smudge. He was trying unsuccessfully to get Smudge to push a small, round stone into a hole, a feat that most snails had no problem with. Smudge, however, was a little slower than most snails and continued to ignore Ribbit's request, choosing to slide in circles instead. His parents were at work and Zippy was at a Dandelion Girls meeting, discussing their upcoming cookie sales, so Ribbit was alone at the house. As much as Ribbit loved his sister, it was nice to have a little time to himself, and Zippy absolutely loved being a Dandelion Girl and couldn't wait to go to their weekly meetings.

Ribbit looked up from Smudge's pathetic display and saw his mother approaching, mumbling something quietly to herself.

"Hey, Ma!" he jumped up, leaving Smudge to his dizzying charade.

"Oh, hello Ribbykins. I didn't see you there," she said in a somber tone, looking down at her toes.

"What's wrong, Ma?" Ribbit asked, raising his brow and reaching out to grab his mother's fingers.

"Oh, I'm just a little worried because I haven't been able to catch many flies with my little ones at school this week," she sighed.

"That's okay, Ma. You're probably just having a bad week. I'm sure next week will be better and you'll catch lots of flies," Ribbit assured her. He'd never seen his mother so upset before, and this was the first time, since he was a tadpole, that she had not come home with any flies. She was, after all, the best fly-catching teacher in all of Lily Pad Hollow.

"No, Ribbit. I don't think you understand. It's not that I am having difficulty catching flies. The problem is that there are no—" She stopped mid-sentence.

Ribbit scrutinized his mother's face. *No what? No what?* He wondered.

His mother saw his worry and she quickly lifted her face into a crooked grin. She gently touched Ribbit on the chin, turning his face up to hers. "I'm sorry, little one. Everything is just fine. I'm just having a tough day, that's all. Nothing you need to worry about. How about we go to the Backwater Café and get you a mosquito sundae? How does that sound?"

He hesitated because he knew that something was wrong. However, he never turned down a mosquito sundae, so he nodded his head and smiled back up at his mother, her hand still under his chin.

"Great. Why don't you be a dear and put Smudge in his pen while I put my things away and we'll get going?" The crooked smile was still plastered on her smooth, freckle-less face. Sometimes when he looked at her flawless complexion, he wondered where Zippy got all of her freckles. Neither his mother nor his father had many of them. It must have been just one of those weird hidden family traits or something.

Doing as he was told, he managed to get Smudge to stop skating in circles long enough to lock him up in his pen, being sure to give him an algae treat and a pat on the head before saying good-bye. He still felt uneasy as he walked around the house. He paused a moment to look out across the motionless pond, noticing that it was eerily quiet. He began to wonder what was going on. He knew that something was really worrying his mother, but what could it be? Why couldn't his mother catch flies this week?

Just then, his mother closed the front door softly behind her and turned to Ribbit. She wore a big straw sunhat and carried a matching purse, along with a giant grin meant to assure him that everything was fine.

"Are you ready, my little tadpole?"

Ribbit nodded and the two of them headed out.

They made their way down the main street of town, not uttering a single word to each other. Outside of his hardware store,

Mr. Boing teetered on a tall ladder, hanging a new sign above his door. He caught sight of them as they walked by and scrambled down the ladder to greet them. Ribbit's father was a regular customer at the hardware store, so a close friendship had blossomed with Mr. Boing over the years. The smell of rocks and wood chips reminded Ribbit of the many afternoons he'd spent in the shop with his father picking out tools and supplies for his various projects.

"Hello, Flora. How's Springer doing? Haven't seen him around the shop in quite a while," Mr. Boing said as he stepped down from the last rung of the ladder. He fixed his blue hat and adjusted the straps on his overalls as he approached them.

"Yes, well, he's been a little preoccupied lately. I'm sure he'll be back in no time to buy new tools for the next project he sets his mind on." His mother laughed.

"Well I hope so." He crouched down and patted Ribbit on the head. "Hello there, Ribbit. What are you two up to?"

"We're going to the Backwater Café for a mosquito sundae," Ribbit smiled. It was hard to pretend that his mind wasn't totally preoccupied with his mother's strange behavior. Usually he would have been thrilled to go for a sundae, but today just wasn't the same. He was sure that Mr. Boing knew him well enough by now that he could see right through his phony enthusiasm.

"Well, then. I hope that all works out. It was nice seeing you both. Tell Springer I said hello." He tipped his hat and mounted his ladder to finish his task, as Ribbit and his mother resumed their silent walk down Main Street.

What did he mean, "hope it all works out"? Ribbit wonder-ed. *What an odd thing to say about getting a sundae.*

As they stepped into the café, they were greeted by the chim-ing of the bells on the front door and the delicious aroma of candied insects and fresh moss. At the counter, on two of the bright red stoo-ls, sat Mr. BugEye and his son, Pickles. At the sound of the bells jingling, Mr. BugEye turned toward the door and nodded at Ribbit and his mother. Pickles, on the other hand, continued eating his candy-coated insect, which had turned his lips a neon shade of blue. He wore a bright, multicolored baseball cap that had shades of green like his skin, red like the stool he sat on, and blue like his lips, making him blend in perfectly with his surroundings. It was almost as if he had planned it.

Behind the counter was the familiar face of Mr. Boggy, the owner and top chef of the Backwater Café. Just the sight of Mr. Boggy's worn, wrinkled face usually made Ribbit's heart skip a beat with joy and anticipation of the treats to come. However, something about Mr. Boggy's face wasn't the same today. His expression look-ed heavy, his wrinkles more noticeable and his words of welcome not so convincing.

"Good day, Mr. Boggy. How are you today, old friend?" his mother asked, nodding her head and offering up a pleasant smile.

"Hello, Mrs. McFly and Ribbit," Mr. Boggy said, offering a gentle smile in return before whispering, "I wish I could say that all was well, but unfortunately we are barely making it through."

"I know what you mean," his mother whispered. Then she glanced down at Ribbit, the worry reappearing on her face. "Little Ribbit would like to have a mosquito sundae, Mr. Boggy. Is there any way that you could scoop one together for my little boy?"

Mr. Boggy came out from behind the counter and crouched down to Ribbit's level. Then he looked Ribbit straight in the eyes and grabbed Ribbit's fingers in his. "I'm sorry, my boy, but we are all out of mosquito sundaes." He glanced up at Ribbit's mother with a look of sorrow and regret. "How about a nice crunchy candied water strider instead? How does that sound?"

No more mosquito sundaes? Ribbit's heart sank and his head dropped in disappointment. Candied water striders were not his first choice in candy. In fact, it may have been his last choice, since water striders didn't have that same delightful taste as flies or mosquitoes. They were bitter and, in his opinion, were an insect that did not belong in candy form. However, he could tell by the look on the adults' faces that something big was going on, so he decided to nod his head and pretend for their sake that he was happy to eat a candied water strider.

As Mr. Boggy stood up and headed back behind the counter, Ribbit looked around the store, which seemed much different than usual. Mr. Boggy always had shelves filled with candies and treats, yet today his store was nearly empty. What happened to all of his treats? Why, for the first time since Ribbit could remember, was he all out of mosquito sundaes?

Mr. Boggy retrieved the only jar on a near empty shelf. He

30

slowly opened it and pulled out a small, glossy, bright red candied water strider for Ribbit. Then he handed Ribbit his "treat," closed up the big jar, and put it back up on the shelf.

Ribbit thanked Mr. Boggy before his mother asked him to "be a dear" and sit at the table outside while she had a talk with Mr. Boggy. He knew that she wanted to talk to him about something she didn't want Ribbit to hear about, which, of course, made him want to hear it that much more. So he carefully crept outside, leaving the door open just a sliver, so he could overhear their conversation. He knew that he shouldn't listen in, but his curiosity got the best of him. Something was wrong and he had to know what it was.

After straining his little ears, Ribbit was able to make out some key words in their conversation. "No more flies . . .", ". . . mosquitoes gone, too," and ". . . Lily Pad Hollow in trouble."

His eyes grew wide with fear and panic. His thoughts were frantic. *No more flies? No more mosquitoes? It couldn't be! What are we going to do? Most of the food in Lily Pad Hollow is made from flies and mosquitoes. There aren't enough minnows in the lake to feed all of the frogs of Lily Pad Hollow forever. What are they going to do when the minnows run out? Where are all the flies and mosquitoes?*

Questions clouded his mind like a tropical storm. He began to feel dizzy and he suddenly felt like he had to get away. In a whirl, he dropped his candied water strider, letting it crash into shiny red shards, and hopped away as quickly as his twiggy legs would take him.

He didn't know where he was headed; he just knew that he had to go somewhere. He couldn't sit still knowing that everyone in Lily Pad Hollow was in trouble. As he sprinted through town, Croak spotted him from his front yard. He was swinging gleefully on the swing that hung from the large willow tree in front of his small wooden cottage. Croak called out and waved hello, but Ribbit completely ignored him. He had no time for frogs who were unaware of the trouble their town was in and he was in no mood to talk. So he kept on hopping, leaving Croak swinging behind him, looking annoyed and confused.

After hopping for what seemed like days, he ended up at the shallows near the cattail borders, puzzled and out of breath. He stopped at the edge of the pond, holding his chest and gasping for air as he sat staring blankly at the peaceful pond with a troubled heart. The season was showing signs of change, and a sprinkling of the leaves overhead were outlined in shades of gold and amber. This was usually Ribbit's favorite time of the year, but he couldn't enjoy any of the beauty today.

The words echoed in his mind: "No flies . . . no mosquitoes . . . Lily Pad Hollow in trouble . . ." His eyes welled up with tears. It was only after his heart slowed its rapid beating and his breathing became slower and deeper that he began to cry. For the first time in his life, he no longer felt safe and free from worry in Lily Pad Hollow.

As he wept by the side of the pond, the warm summer breeze whistled its way across the pond, causing the cattails to once again take up their graceful summer dance. The swaying cattails caught his eye, hypnotizing him once more with their beautiful waltz and transforming his sobs into more of a soft whimper. As Ribbit wiped the tears that ran down his cheek, he was suddenly struck with an idea.

Maybe this is it! He thought. *My chance to show Lily Pad Hollow what I am made of!* His pulse quickened and he felt the corners of his mouth curl up into a smile. Just then, he knew what had to be done. He was going to travel outside the cattail borders of Lily Pad Hollow and save the day.

A Young Frog with a Crazy Dream

After contemplating his noble plan for some time, Ribbit decided to head home. He knew his mother was probably worried sick about him since he dashed away from the Backwater Café in such a hurry and with no explanations.

As he neared the walkway that led home, he could hear the faint sound of voices coming from his house.

"Do you have any idea where he could be?" his mother asked.

"Nope. Last I saw him he was leaping like a mad frog, his eyes looking all crazy and stuff." Ribbit knew that had to be Croak and he could only imagine the frenzy he was about to walk into.

He took a deep breath, bracing himself for the chaos that was sure to come, as he slowly slid the door open. As soon as the door made its familiar squeak, his mother darted to Ribbit and engulfed him in a warm embrace, kissing every little spot on his froggy face.

"Oh, my Ribbykins! I was so worried about you!" She said. Then, almost as quickly as she had latched on to him, his mother's mood changed from relief to rage. "Where have you been?" she demanded, squishing his face in her hands, her intense stare searing into his eyes. "Do you know what you have put us through? You left without any explanation!" Her hands shook and her voice trembled with anger.

"I know, I know, Ma," he said. "I've, I've . . ." He gulped, trying to avoid his mother's burning stare. "I've been at the cattail borders."

His mother let his face out of her grip and began flailing her arms up in the air, fluttering like an angry bird, and shouted, "Why on earth would you suddenly up and leave just to go to the cattail borders?" Then, she put her hands firmly on her hips, letting Ribbit know without any mistake that she was furious, and demanded an explanation.

Ribbit stared silently back at his mother, not knowing what to say. Should he tell her the truth or should he just make up a story about chasing a big fly, or seeing a friend, so that she wouldn't have to worry?

"Well?" she asked sternly.

After a few seconds of ping ponging between the truth and a lie, he decided to go with the truth. "I heard what you and Mr. Boggy said in the café," he blurted.

His mother's left hand dropped from her hip and her right hand shot up to her chest, clutching her heart in disbelief. "You what?" she murmured in a soft voice, her eyes meeting his once more.

"I heard what you were talking about, Ma. I know about the flies and the mosquitoes and the trouble we're all in." This time, Ribbit spoke in a softer tone, too. He knew his response would upset her. He looked over to his right and saw a bewildered Croak, who stood with his mouth wide open and his hands hung loosely by his side. Ribbit had completely forgotten that he was standing there and he felt sorry to see his friend go from being a lighthearted, cheerful frog to feeling just as troubled as he was. Although part of him was glad to have his friend in on the big secret, another part of him also wished that Croak didn't have to be involved and could go on believing that Lily Pad Hollow was a peaceful, carefree place to be, like he himself had thought not too long ago.

"Oh, Ribbykins," his mother whispered quietly as she grasped her son in a warm embrace. "I'm so sorry you had to hear that, my little tadpole." She gently let go of her embrace and held Ribbit by the shoulders. She stared deep into his eyes. "I promise you, honey, this is nothing that you have to worry about. Your father and I will make sure that everything will be alright."

"That's just it, Ma. There's nothing that you and Dad can do from here," he said. He wasn't going to let her give him any false hopes. He wasn't a tadpole anymore and he was smart enough to know that this problem was bigger than his parents.

"Whatever do you mean? We can live off of water striders and minnows until the flies and mosquitoes return."

"What if they never return, Ma? Then what? We just sit around here and starve to death? There aren't enough minnows to feed us all here forever!"

"Ribbit, you're getting way ahead of yourself here, son. You're just a young frog and shouldn't worry yourself with such things. I told you that your father and I will handle this situation . . ."

"Did you even take a minute to think about why the flies and mosquitoes aren't coming here anymore? There has to be a reason, Ma. Don't you want to know why?" Ribbit interrupted.

"Sure I do, honey, but there is nothing that we ordinary frogs can do. We'll just have to leave it up to the town officials to figure out what is best for us. Until they figure out a plan, all we can do is make the best out of the situation," she said.

"So what you're saying is that we're just supposed to sit around and wait for Mayor Cornelius to come up with a solution? The frog has never set foot outside of our borders. How could he possibly figure out what's going on?" He was getting so riled up that he was pacing, flailing his hands in the air, and beginning to shout.

"Ribbit, mind your place," his mother responded in a stern voice. He could tell that she was not happy with his outburst. "We have all put faith in Mayor Cornelius to do what's right for us. There's no use in getting all worked up when we don't even know what his plans are. Your father is at a town meeting right now getting information from the Mayor on what to do about this problem. So let's just wait until he gets home to hear what our next moves are."

His mother went into the kitchen, grabbed a sponge, and began scrubbing the sink. Ribbit could see the worry, frustration, and concern that his mother was feeling by the way she was scrubbing anxiously in the same spot over and over again. Seeing his mother so upset broke his heart, so he decided to soften his approach.

"I'm sorry for upsetting you, Ma. I'm just worried that's all. I think we really need to send someone beyond the borders to figure out what is going on. I just don't see what good it is going to do to sit around here guessing what's wrong," he said softly.

His mother stopped her anxious scrubbing and turned to her son, a look of sorrow in her eyes. "I know you're worried, but I don't want you to concern yourself with such grown-up matters. Now, be a dear and run outside and play with your friend Croak. Your sister will be home from Dandelion Girls soon, and I don't want her to hear about any of this."

He could sense his mother's desperation. He really didn't want to upset her anymore and he definitely didn't want Zippy to know what was going on, so he agreed. He grabbed a dazed Croak, who hadn't moved an inch or spoken a word since Ribbit's arrival, by the arm and led him out the door.

*****

The two friends sat side by side in total silence for about an hour, gazing out on the still pond, their minds a flurry of thoughts and emotions. Ribbit turned to his friend and finally spoke out.

"I'm sorry you had to be dragged into this, Croak." Croak didn't even flinch at his words and continued staring wide-eyed at the pond. "I really wish that you didn't have to hear about the trouble we're all in. That's why I ignored you earlier when you were swinging in your front yard. I didn't want you to know about the flies."

Croak turned his head toward Ribbit, his wide eyes still staring, before returning his gaze to the motionless pond ahead. He didn't have to say anything. Ribbit knew what he was thinking.

"Listen, Croak. Now that we know about this, we have to do something." Again, Croak only stared.

"You know they're never going to send any officials outside the cattail borders. Mayor Cornelius isn't going to go and he surely isn't going to send any of his beloved advisors," he continued, looking down at his webbed toes. He took a deep breath and decided to let Croak in on his plan, even though he wasn't sure how Croak would respond. "So, I'm gonna do it, Croak. I'm gonna leave Lily Pad Hollow and figure out what happened to our flies and mosquitoes."

Croak snapped out of his trance and shot a quick glance at Ribbit. "You've got to be kidding me?"

"No, I'm not! You know this is what I've always dreamed about. I'm going to go out there and save Lily Pad Hollow." He could feel the excitement welling up inside him. Until he actually said the words, the whole thing didn't seem real.

Croak stared deep into Ribbit's eyes, his face drooping with disapproval. "You've officially lost it, Ribbit. There's no way you're gonna to make it outside the cattail borders. Are you crazy? You wanna die or something?"

"No, of course I don't want to die. I just want to do something great for once. But thanks for the vote of approval, Croak. Glad to know that you're on my side," he said sarcastically. Croak was acting just like everyone else who didn't believe in him. He stood up and began to walk away. He'd had a rough day and couldn't stand any more criticism or doubt, especially not from the one person that he thought would be on his side.

"Come on, Rib! You know that's not it," Croak said, grabbing his hand and stopping him from leaving. "It's just that we're young frogs. What do we know? We've never even had to make our own dinners or been in a fight. I mean, I haven't even taken a girl out on a date and neither have you. So what makes you think we could make it outside the borders?"

His heart sank. Was Croak right? Was he completely insane for thinking he could leave Lily Pad Hollow? All those things he said were true. There were a lot of things that he had never done, so what made him think that he could do something so great? Something that no other frog in Lily Pad Hollow has ever been able to do? What made him so special? Maybe that was it. Maybe he wasn't special. Maybe he was just an ordinary young frog who was only good at imaginary battles and nothing more.

He swiftly pulled his hand away from Croak's, his face heavy with rejection, before hopping back to his house.

"Ribbit! Don't be like this! Come on!" Croak shouted, as Ribbit disappeared into his house, slamming the door behind him.

He rushed into his room, avoiding his mother's questions. He locked himself in his bedroom, away from the world, away from Croak. Completely discouraged and heartbroken, he flopped onto his bed and began to cry. He would have expected someone like Squiggy or Kilroy to destroy his dreams and make him feel like he wasn't good enough, but he never expected Croak to make him feel that way. Somehow, he always imagined that Croak and Phinn believed that he could do anything and would be the only two frogs in the whole pond who would support him no matter what. For the first time, he felt completely alone.

After sobbing for a few minutes, he closed his eyes and dozed off to sleep. He awoke with a start at the sound of his parents' muffled voices coming from the living room. He quietly crept to the door and opened it a sliver, trying his best to listen closely without being noticed. They were talking about the town meeting his father had attended and what Mayor Cornelius had planned to save Lily Pad Hollow.

"Mayor Cornelius said that we should all just sit tight and wait for the flies to return. He clearly doesn't want to send anyone outside the borders. We can see only a little beyond the borders from our border patrol station, so that's not going to be of much help. He

---

41

thinks that it's too risky to send anyone out there when none of us knows what's going on," his father said in a hushed tone.

"Are we really just supposed to sit here and twiddle our thumbs just hoping that the flies will come back? What if they don't, Springer? What if something's going on out there and they don't come back? What then?" Ribbit could tell his mother was starting to panic, the same way that he had panicked when he heard the news at the café.

"Flora, you and I both know that this is out of our hands. We have to just trust Mayor Cornelius's plan and do what we are told." His father sounded defeated, something Ribbit had never heard in his father's voice before.

Ribbit gently shut his door and uncovered his firefly nightlight. His mind raced and his heart beat violently in his chest. He had to come up with a plan to save Lily Pad Hollow, and if Croak and Phinn weren't going to help him, then he was just going to have to do it on his own.

That's What Friends Are For

After staying up most of the night thinking about his plans for escape, Ribbit was able to drift off for only a few hours before awaking to the familiar sound of his cricket alarm chirping loudly, announcing that a new day was beginning. He flicked the jar containing the wake-up cricket, and lay in bed, staring at the ceiling and wondering what his adventure was going to be like.

Before long, he could hear his mother clanging around in the kitchen, preparing breakfast and humming her familiar tune. He could also hear Zippy's little voice chiming in and singing along, making up words as she went. Suddenly, his heart felt heavy with guilt. In all of his planning last night, he'd never stopped to think about the effect his plan would have on his family. How would they feel about him going on such a dangerous adventure?

He sprung out of bed and quickly tucked all of his escape plans in one of his school books, *The Physics of Lily Pad Leaping*, so that they wouldn't be found. That was Ribbit's favorite hiding place to stash his secret letters and imaginary treasure maps because no one in their right mind cared to read about the physics of leaping from lily pad to lily pad—boring! He knew that he had to leave for his big journey soon and couldn't risk anyone (especially Zippy) finding out about it and spoiling his plans.

After all the evidence was tucked squarely away, he joined his sister and parents in the kitchen for a disappointing breakfast of warm moss-meal and boiled minnows. His parents tried to put on a happy face and disguise their concern. He did his best to pretend to enjoy his tasteless minnow breakfast as well. Zippy, on the other hand, was not so tactful.

"Yuck! This tastes terrible!" she blurted as she spat out her food.

"I'm sorry you don't like it, Zippy-Lou, but it's all that we have for now," Ribbit's mother said as she picked at her own stringy, lumpy moss.

"Oh, it's not that bad, little one. Eat up so that you will grow to be big and strong," his father added, though his words seemed to be of no encouragement as Zippy continued to push her food around on her plate.

Once they finished their unpleasant meal, his parents gave their son a big slimy kiss before they both headed off to another town meeting. Ribbit was given strict instructions to watch Zippy and complete some chores before having Phinn and Croak come over to play. He couldn't believe it. His mother actually said the word *play*! In a time like this! The last thing he wanted to do was play. Plan, organize, orchestrate, yes . . . but definitely not play. Anyway, he had no desire to meet up with his friends because Croak had already made him feel crummy about his plans, and he was sure that Phinn would do the same.

After a few hours of scrubbing, sweeping, and cleaning, there was a gentle knock on the front door.

"Ooh! Let me get it!" Zippy exclaimed as she dropped the rag she was using to wipe down the table and bounded toward the door.

"Oh no you don't. We don't know who it is. It could be a stranger, Zippy. I'll get it." He put down his broom and hopped to the door, knowing it had to be Croak and Phinn. Sure enough, he was right. He slowly opened the door to face his friends.

"Ribbit, can we talk to you for a minute?" Phinn asked. A shy and nervous Croak stood behind him on the front step.

"Umm . . . I guess," Ribbit shrugged holding the door open. They hopped into the living room and took a seat on the big comfy couch where they'd held pretend sword fights too many times to count.

He gently closed the door and took a deep breath. "Hey, Zippy. Could you give us a minute and go play with your Polly Polliwogs in your room?"

"Aw, do I have to?" Zippy whined, looking disappointed. As much as she adored dressing up her Pollies and playing house with them, she really just wanted to hang out with the boys.

"Just for a little bit. Then I will play Pollies with you, okay?"

"Promise?" she asked, her big eyes staring up at Ribbit.

"I promise." He patted her gently on the head. He was always a sucker for those eyes.

"Okay, Ribbit," she said as she hopped down the hallway and into her room. He felt sorry to have sent her away, but he knew that he had some important business to discuss with his friends.

Part of him was really afraid of what they were going to say to him. Since Phinn was with Croak he was sure Croak had spilled the beans about their discussion yesterday, and as much as he wanted to pretend that he didn't care what his friends thought about his plans, the truth was their opinions meant more to him than anyone else's.

Once they heard the door shut to Zippy's room, Phinn spoke up. "Rib, Croak told me all about your plan and I have to say that it sounds completely mad," he said, as Croak nodded his head in agreement. "We know you've always dreamed of going on a big ad-venture and stuff, but come on Rib, this plan is absolutely insane! We're just little frogs, for pond's sake. What can we do?" Phinn looked at him with sincere concern, but that didn't ease the pain of his words. He didn't believe in Ribbit either.

"I just want to do something great, guys. Lily Pad Hollow is in trouble and this is my time to show everyone what I'm made of.

Sure, I'm not the biggest frog, or the smartest frog, or even the most athletic frog, but I am willing to give it a try, which is more than I can say for anyone else." He was beginning to yell.

"But, Rib, you heard what the Mayor said. He doesn't want anyone trying to cross the borders. It's too dangerous because we don't know what's out there. No one knows what's out there. Are you really willing to risk that? I mean are you really willing to risk your life for this, Ribbit, because that's what you'd be doing?" Phinn was always the voice of reason in the group and he did have a point. This adventure was going to be dangerous and life threatening.

Ribbit appreciated that his friends cared so much for him that they would try and talk him out of going, but he also knew what had to be done.

"I can't sit here and let this town and all of the good frogs living here go under because our Mayor isn't brave enough to get to the bottom of this problem and work on a solution. So, the answer to your question, my friend, is yes, I know that this journey's going to be a dangerous one and yes, I'm willing to risk it."

Croak unfolded himself from the little ball he had been sitting in and exchanged a weary glance with Phinn. "We had a feeling you would say that, but we had to try and talk you out of it. As much as you know I don't agree with you, Ribbit, if this is something that is as important as you say, and that you really want to do, we're with you, buddy."

Ribbit's eyes grew wide with excitement. "You mean, you mean . . ."

"Yep," Croak blurted.

"Yes, Rib, we're going with you. That's what friends are for," Phinn smiled.

Ribbit stared at his two best friends in the whole wide world and knew that he could not love them more. He bounced over to his friends, knocking them over on the couch and embracing them tighter than he ever had before.

"I'm so excited, I feel like my heart's gonna explode!" He shouted, playfully wrestling with his friends in a fit of laughter.

"Alright, alright! We can't have that happen or we won't get anywhere," Phinn giggled, as the three boys wrestled, nearly knocking over Ribbit's mother's fancy carved reed vase.

Croak stopped roughhousing for a moment, gave Ribbit an apologetic look, and muttered, "Sorry about yesterday, Rib. I shouldn't have doubted you."

"Aw, it's alright, you big lug," he teased, hitting Croak in the arm. "All that matters is that you came around."

"Okay, okay guys. We have some planning to do. When are we leaving, Ribbit?" the voice of reason chimed in again.

"Oh, I almost forgot! I have the plans in my room. We leave tomorrow morning, before dawn." Ribbit leapt to his room, pulled out the plans, and shared them with his nervous, but excited, companions, going over every detail of how they would avoid being seen by the Border Patrol and getting the supplies they needed.

After tedious planning and preparing, Phinn and Croak headed home to get ready for the adventure they were about to embark on. They agreed not to tell anyone about their plans, so no-one stood in their way. It was going to be their secret; the biggest secret they would ever share. Ribbit hopped for joy in his room, overwhelmed with excitement for the big day ahead, and then he joined Zippy in her room to play Pollies with her as he had promised. Life as he knew it was about to change.

The Great Escape

Ribbit lay awake all night listening to the familiar sound of crickets in the distance and the much closer sound of his father croaking in his sleep. He was way too excited to sleep. He knew that everything was ready to go. He had packed all of his supplies, including his favorite book and firefly nightlight, and had written his parents a long letter about his journey, telling them not to worry and that he would make them proud. Even though he was all set to go, he kept reviewing his checklist in his head over and over again. He knew if he forgot anything, there was no going back. He also had no clue what he was going to face out there in the world and he wanted to be prepared for anything he may come across. He hoped that Croak and Phinn did the same and he was sure they weren't resting any easier than he was.

Before he knew it, the quiet chirping of his cricket alarm went off, signaling that it was time to go. He couldn't remember the last time he had woken up before dawn, but he never felt more awake in his life. He quickly gathered all of his belongings, going over his checklist once again, and then made his bed and set out the letter to his parents. He knew how worried they would be about him when they woke up in the morning and found him gone, but he also knew how important it was for him to go on this journey and he was sure they would thank him later on.

Before heading out the door, he stopped by Zippy's room to say good-bye. He crept softly in her room, being careful not to bump into her big Polliwog Pad, which was home for all her Pollies, or her giant purple rocking goldfish toy. When he finally made it to her bed, he sat down gently beside his snoozing sister and lightly tapped her shoulder to wake her up.

"Hey Zippy, wake up," he whispered, as a groggy Zippy mumbled something he couldn't understand. It kind of sounded like, "Riggor zima noof," which made him giggle. Then, remembering the task at hand, he straightened up and whispered, "Zippy, I'm gonna be gone for a little while. Tell Mom and Dad not to worry about me. Be good and take care of Smudge for me, okay?"

"Okay, Ribbit," Zippy murmured, even though he was sure she was still asleep.

"I'll miss you," he whispered as he leaned in and kissed his sister on her polka-dotted head and tiptoed out her bedroom door.

After quietly sneaking out of his house, he went around back and hugged his favorite little snail good-bye, feeding him one last algae treat, and telling him to be good while he was away. Looking into Smudge's big, bulging eyes made him feel a pang of sadness as he patted the snail's slimy head before heading out to meet his friends and begin his whirlwind adventure.

*****

He breathed in the fresh morning air as he hopped swiftly through a deserted Main Street. It was eerie to see a town, that was usually so alive with the sounds of frogs shopping and young frogs playing, be so empty and still. He took a moment to look one last time at the old Backwater Café, Mr. Boing's hardware store, Dragonfly Elementary, and the pond where he had spent so many endless days splashing and playing around. He closed his eyes and took a deep breath, as if saying good-bye to his beloved town, and hopped onward to the cattail borders to meet up with Croak and Phinn.

By the time he arrived at the edge of the pond, Croak and Phinn were already there, each wearing a nervous smile and greeting him with frantic waves.

"Hi, guys!" he called out in hushed excitement so as not to alert the Border Patrol. "Ready to go?"

"Yep," Croak smiled.

"I think so. You sure you still want to do this?" Phinn asked uneasily.

"Absolutely," he grinned.

"Alright then, Captain, lead the way," Phinn said gently patting Ribbit on the back.

"Okay, guys. The Border Patrol always takes a two-minute break when they are switching shifts from the night shift to the day shift, just before daybreak. That means we have to watch the patrol frogs that are stationed up on that boulder to the left, and as soon as we see them leave their post, we have to act quickly," he whispered. "When I give you the signal, like this . . ." he said, twirling his long, skinny finger in the air, "it means that it is time to move. Got it?"

"Got it!" the two frogs responded, nodding their heads, their wide eyes not even blinking.

"Alright, if my calculations from what you told me are correct," Phinn said, staring up at the stars above and counting methodically to himself, "the patrol's two-minute break should be starting in approximately five minutes."

"Great, that gives us just enough time to go over supplies and put them in my pack. Phinn, did you bring the food?" Ribbit asked, opening his pack and moving the items around to make room.

"Yeah, but we only had minnow sandwiches," his nose crinkled in disgust.

"Well, I guess it's better than nothing," Ribbit shrugged.

"I also brought my magnifying stone and some small empty jars to collect samples of the plant life and whatever else we find," Phinn smiled excitedly. "I'll keep them with me in my pocket though, just in case. Don't want to lose these bad boys."

"Okay," Ribbit rolled his eyes. "Croak, what did you bring?"

"Uh, we didn't have much food left in the house, but I was able to sneak out some water-strider chips."

"Good work, Croak." Ribbit patted him gently on the back. Croak's family didn't have much and Ribbit knew how much that bothered him.

Just then, the patrolfrog's cricket alarm chimed, signifying the end of their shift. In a matter of seconds, the Border Patrol had cleared.

Ribbit sprang into action, giving the hand motion and wading out into the chilly waters of the pond toward the cattail borders. Luckily, the water was shallow and they could walk all the way to the borders with their heads and shoulders above water. His heart was in his throat and his knees were trembling, as his two best buddies followed carefully behind him. As he approached the sleeping cattails, a shiver jolted down his body. For a moment, he felt like turning around and hopping back to the safety of his warm, comfortable home, but he knew his mission was too important and it was too late to turn back now. Before he knew it, they were standing directly in front of the cattails. He took one last deep breath, closed his eyes, and pushed forward. The three brave, young frogs disappeared into the thick cluster of motionless cattails. They had officially left Lily Pad Hollow behind and ventured into the unknown.

The Outside World

The cattails brushed against Ribbit's skin, like many soft, velvety fingers welcoming him into the unknown. He began to notice he could no longer hear any of the familiar sounds of Lily Pad Hollow. The only sounds he could hear now were the sloshing of their feet, the swishing of the cattails, and the pounding of his heart. He decided that they were far away enough to take out his firefly nightlight from his backpack and uncover it so that they could see where they were headed.

In the dim morning light ahead of him, he could make out a clearing behind a wall of reeds shooting up from the muddy waters and creating a curtain of wooden rods. He was glad that he could only see a few feet ahead of him. That way, it wasn't as overwhelming as if the whole, wide world just opened up beyond the borders.

Once he got to the clearing, he took a deep breath. This was it. He had always been able to see the cattail borders, but never beyond. Crossing the reeds would be officially taking him out of the world he knew. Tightening his gut, he led the way into the reeds, which were not as soft and gentle as the cattails had been. The air smelled different among the reeds. It didn't have the same sweet aroma of water lilies, but had more of a musky, woody smell that he had never smelled before. He was glad to smell something new, even if it wasn't as pleasant as water lilies. He took in a deep breath of its woody aroma as he bravely led his friends forward. They hadn't uttered a word since passing through the cattail borders, through the dirt and the muck of the reeds. They simply followed him as if they were his shadow.

"How ya doing back there, guys?" he asked over his shoulder once he felt that they were far enough away from the Border Patrol to be heard.

"I'm okay," mumbled Croak, sounding a little disgruntled.

"I still can't believe that you actually talked us into doing this!" Phinn huffed, scanning cautiously around him as if a predator was about to pounce at any moment. He should have been more focused on where he was walking because he stumbled on a reed and fell face first into the shallow water. He quickly shot up and regained his stepping as if nothing had happened.

"Do you guys realize that we've gone where no frog has gone before? Even R.T. Hopkins never mentioned anything about this!" Ribbit asked as he began marching like an explorer, raising his hand up high in the sky and snubbing his nose at the world.

"You know what? You're absolutely right, Ribbit," Phinn agreed. "And being that we are the first frogs to pass through this route, it only seems fitting that we should name this place. You know, so that we can describe it to the other frogs when we get back." For the first time, Phinn actually sounded excited and although Ribbit couldn't see his face in the dim light, he knew that Phinn was smiling.

"Phinny, my boy, you are on to something. Since you came up with the idea, why don't you name it?" Ribbit called out behind him.

"How about Reedville?" Croak chimed in.

"Umm . . . not quite right, Croak. It needs to be catchier," Phinn scoffed.

"How about Reedtopia?" Ribbit spoke out after a few minutes of silence.

"Ah . . . you're getting closer. It's still not quite right yet," Phinn replied, deep in thought.

"I've got it!" Phinn finally shouted. "The Great Reed Barrier!" He bellowed in a deep, dramatic tone fit for something grand.

"The Great Reed Barrier!" Both Ribbit and Croak giggled, high fiving each other with delight.

"It's perfect, Phinn!" Ribbit hollered. "Good work, my friend. The Great Reed Barrier it is! Now onward through The Great

———

Reed Barrier!" He could hardly contain his excitement to be out in the world, exploring.

The brave adventurers hiked for what seemed like forever, through boundless rows of sharp, pointy reeds. They hadn't come across a single creature yet, which, in Ribbit's opinion, was a good thing. It wasn't until the sun was higher and the sky painted a pale cotton candy pink, that the boys could see far enough through the thicket of reeds to an opening up ahead.

"Wahoo!" Croak shouted. "Land ho!"

All three frogs quickened their pace so they could get to the clearing and take a well-needed rest. When Ribbit pushed aside the last reed, he came to a stop and gasped.

"What's the hold up?" Phinn said irritably.

"Yeah, what's the deal?" an annoyed Croak added.

Ribbit turned back to his friends with large, wondering eyes and whispered, "You've gotta see this!"

And with that, he moved aside, giving his friends a clear view of a glittering, rushing river.

"What is it?" Croak whispered, as if the river could hear him.

"It's a river, genius," Phinn said as he elbowed Croak in the arm.

"Ha ha! He wasn't lying! I knew it! R.T. Hopkins was telling the truth about rivers!" Ribbit exclaimed, his eyes glued on the rushing water. In the Hollow, rivers were dismissed by most as a product of R.T. Hopkins' imagination, and yet, there it was, living proof that R.T. Hopkins was true to his word.

The boys looked at each other and began hooting and hollering with delight. Ribbit started doing cartwheels around and around in the dirt before falling over with dizziness. Croak wildly punched the air, crying out, "Yeah! Yeah! Yeah!" while Phinn danced eccentrically to the tune of his own beat. They had really made it! They were living the dream!

Before long, the sun was blazing brightly in the vivid blue sky. All of their celebrating left them exhausted and gasping for air as they fell to the ground.

"Can you believe it, guys? Can you believe that we're really here?" Ribbit panted, squinting at a fluffy white cloud that he swore resembled a lily pad.

"I know! This is the life!" Phinn added, his hands resting behind his head and his face aglow with happiness.

"I never expected anything like this. I mean, I knew we'd see something cool, but not a freakin' river!" Croak exclaimed, still trying to catch his breath from all the activity.

Ribbit turned to his friends, sat up, and gently tapped them both on the shoulders so they would fix their eyes on him for a moment. "Hey, thanks for coming with me. It really means a lot."

"We know, Ribbit," Phinn said with a warm smile.

"Like we were going to let you have all this fun without us!" Croak joked, as they shared in a good laugh. "Alright, alright, enough of this sappy stuff. I'm starving. Let's eat."

Ribbit opened up his pack and took out a lunch of minnow sandwiches (yuck!) and crunchy water strider chips, which they quickly gobbled down. He stared out on the broad, winding river, its waters flowing to some unknown place. A place that Ribbit hoped he would get to see sooner than later.

A Stranger Creeping in the Reeds

Once their bellies were full and they had finished off the crumbs from the water strider chips, it was time for the three frogs to come up with a plan for where to go next on their great adventure.

"Well, I think we need to swim through the river and go to the other side where those big trees are," Ribbit said, staring way out into the distance. He pointed a skinny finger straight ahead at two full trees that were waving in the slight wind of the warm summer day. They looked like two green umbrellas standing tall and proud.

"Umm . . . Rib, you're forgetting one little detail," Croak said uneasily. "I don't swim!"

How could he have forgotten in all of his scheming and planning that Croak couldn't swim farther than the closest lily pad in the pond, which is a feat most frogs can do their first year of school?

Croak had always had trouble swimming. He claimed that it had something to do with the webbing on one of his feet, but Ribbit suspected that he was more afraid of swimming than he was unable to swim.

"Sorry, bud. Totally forgot. Okay, we're just going to have to figure out another way to get across the river. It looks too deep to wade across. Any suggestions, guys?"

"We could build a raft," Phinn suggested.

"Great idea, Phinny boy! Let's see if we can get enough reeds together to build a raft and float our way across the river." Ribbit scanned the ground, looking around for fallen reeds. Phinn and Croak did the same.

After separating and searching tirelessly across every inch of the river shore, the boys could only gather up three sturdy reeds, which was not nearly enough to build a raft. They were going to have to come up with a new plan.

"Do you think you could pull some reeds out of the ground, Croak?" Phinn asked, knowing that Croak was the strongest of them.

"I could try." Croak hopped over to the nearest reed and began pulling with all of his might. He moaned and he groaned, but the reed wouldn't budge. Defeated and out of breath, he turned back to his friends and shrugged his shoulders.

"So much for that," Ribbit sighed. "Got any more ideas?"

He turned to his companions who looked just as puzzled as he was. They sat along the shore of the rushing river, contemplating their next move. Croak began throwing stones in the river just as he used to at home, while Phinn worked eagerly with the three reeds they had found, unsuccessfully attempting to put together a makeshift raft.

Just then, Ribbit heard a rustling in the reeds behind him. He guessed that Croak and Phinn heard it too because they stopped what they were doing and became as still as tree stumps. He signaled for his friends to come close to him.

"What was that?" Croak whispered hoarsely.

"I don't know, but it was definitely coming from over there." Ribbit pointed a shaky finger at the thick curtain of reeds directly in front of them. "Quick, Phinn, grab the reeds we collected for our raft and we'll use them as a weapons to defend ourselves."

Phinn scampered over to the reeds and swiftly passed one to Ribbit and one to Croak. Ribbit held his reed like a great sword, pointing it at the rustling reeds ahead, while Croak and Phinn held theirs more like baseball bats. They stood closely behind Ribbit, motionless and as silent as fish.

Ribbit's heart beat so fast it nearly choked him. He had always dreamed of fighting an evil foe and in his imaginary battles he was always brave and menacing. However, now that he faced real-life danger, he found himself to be less sure of himself, and more petrified. He suddenly felt more like a young frog than he ever had before. What had he gotten himself into? What could possibly have made him think that he would be some expert swordsman when his only sword had been a reed or a cattail? The reality of the situation began to sink in as he held up the shaking reed, waiting to meet his fate.

The rustling of the reeds inched closer and closer to the terrified frogs until it was nearly at their feet.

This is it, Ribbit thought. *This is the end of my life. Whatever it is that is out there is going to eat me and that is going to be the end. Why, oh why did I get myself into this? What could I have been thinking? I will never get to see Lily Pad Hollow again and the flies will never return, so my mom will lose her job and all of the frogs will starve. And I didn't even get to figure out what happened to all the flies.*

A veil of tears covered Ribbit's eyes at the thought of what was about to happen. He quickly shook his head, blinking his tears away. This was no time to have a breakdown. This was the time for him to be brave, like he always imagined he would be.

Desperation lent him strength as he tensed up, closed his eyes, furrowed his brow in determination, and lunged at the unseen enemy shouting a piercing, "Hi-ya!" He felt his reed hit something, his arm ricocheting backward from the blow.

I did it! I actually did it! Ha, ha!

And with this joyful thought in mind, he opened his eyes to catch a glimpse of his fallen enemy, not knowing whether it was an alligator or a snake or a fox, or any other predator that he had read about in R.T. Hopkins's stories. But when he opened his eyes wide enough, he saw a creature he never would've expected.

An Unlikely Friend Lends a Hand

"Ow! What was that for?" the creature whined, trying to see if there any been any damage done to the sturdy shell she wore on her back.

Ribbit stood motionless, still clinging on to his mighty reed, his mouth dropped in amazement. He scanned the creature with its scaly skin and brown, spotted shell, which looked as if it were as hard as a rock. What on earth was this thing? He began to panic. Was this something that would try to eat them or was it a friendly creature, like the ducks he had read about in stories? He couldn't be sure.

"Ah, ha! Take that! And there's more where that came from, evil-doer!" Ribbit shouted, flailing his reed around like he used to in his imaginary battles, trying to pretend like he knew what he was doing.

"What are you talking about?" the creature replied, her face squinting in confusion.

"Oh, you can't trick us, you fiend! If you want to eat us, you're gonna have to get to us first!" Phinn shouted, trying to sound dangerous and confident, yet still crouching squarely behind Croak.

"Yep!" Croak added, still holding his reed high in the air like a bat.

Just then, the creature let out a colossal laugh and said, "Eat you? You really think I want to eat you?"

"Well, yes. Don't you?" Ribbit asked, gazing at the creature as if he didn't know what to do next.

"You've got to be kidding me!" the creature scoffed. "Me, eat you? Now that's a laugh! Are you froggies messing with me?" As the creature spoke more, Ribbit began to realize that this was a girl creature, probably around his age, and she didn't sound too threatening. Maybe he could trust her.

"Hey, wait a minute!" Phinn said suspiciously, his face scrunched and his reed pointed sharply at the creature. "How do we know you aren't just trying to trick us into thinking that you don't want to eat us, when you really do want to eat us? Huh? Huh?" He jabbed in her direction.

"Hey, cool it, little froggy!" The creature put her hand up in a gesture to stop. "I'm an Insectarian. My family and I only eat bugs and mollusks, not little froggies like yourselves. Gross. No offense."

"None taken," Ribbit said, as he breathed a sigh of relief and let his reed point down to the ground.

The creature continued. "I mean, don't get me wrong, some turtles would love to eat you little froggies up. But to me, you look about as appealing as a bowl full of mud." A playful smile flickered across her face.

Feeling foolish, Ribbit, Croak, and Phinn put down their weapons and began to chuckle with their new unusual friend.

"You'll have to excuse us," Ribbit said, his face as red as a tomato. "We've never seen anything like you before."

"You mean to tell me you've never seen a turtle before?" she asked, looking at them suspiciously as if she couldn't tell if they were joking or not.

"Fascinating! You're a turtle! A *real* turtle!" Phinn cried, coming out from behind Croak to get a good look at the mysterious creature.

"So they really do exist!" Croak exclaimed, his mouth open and his eyes bulging.

Ribbit's stomach gurgled with excitement. "Wow! I can't believe this! You see, we come from Lily Pad Hollow and no frog there has ever seen a turtle before. I mean, before this very moment, we thought that turtles were mythical creatures that only existed in stories."

"Okay, now you frogs are beginning to freak me out. Are you messing with me? Is this some sort of joke or something?" the turtle asked, watching doubtfully as the three bubbly frogs hopped around her in circles, tapping on her hard beautiful shell.

"No, no! It's not a joke. You really are the first turtle that we've ever seen in our whole lives!" Ribbit exclaimed gleefully.

"Well, then, it's a pleasure to meet you. My name is Shelly." She grinned a wide, toothless grin.

"I'm Ribbit!" he said proudly, pointing his thumb sternly in his chest. "And these are my friends, Phinn and Croak."

"Nice to meet you!" Phinn bowed wearing an impish grin.

"Turtle!" Croak blurted, still in awe of what he was seeing.

"Yes, well. This has been interesting," Shelly said, as she raised her brows and began to walk away. "I gotta be going now. It was nice meeting you Ribbit, Phinn, and . . . what was your name again?"

"You . . . you . . . you're a turtle," Croak sputtered.

"Okay, I'm outta here. See ya froggies!" And with that, Shelly dove into the rushing river and began to swim across. Just then, Ribbit was struck with an idea.

"Wait! Wait! Shelly! Wait a second!" Ribbit called out, waving his twiggy arms, desperately trying to get Shelly's attention.

Shelly heard the commotion, quickly turned around, and paddled back to shore. "What's up, froggies? You see another dangerous predator?" She giggled.

"Shelly, you can swim!" Ribbit exclaimed.

"Umm . . . yeah. I kinda already know that, Ribbit, but thanks for pointing it out." She rolled her eyes and looked at Ribbit as if he was insane. "Is that all or do you want to point out that I can walk and breathe, too?"

"No, no. I just mean that you can swim and we can't exactly make it across the river."

Shelly giggled. "Oh, I gotcha! You want a ride. Hop on, froggies!" Shelly waved a dripping hand, signaling them to jump onto her shell.

"Thanks, Shelly! We really appreciate it," Ribbit said, as he and his friends sprung onto Shelly's back, taking their reeds with them to use as walking sticks or future weapons if need be.

"No prob," Shelly called out. She splashed into the fast moving water and swam her new friends to the other bank of the river. Then she bid them farewell and continued on her way downriver, swimming swiftly with the current.

Once Shelly was out of sight, the three frogs took a look around and began to think about what their next move would be. Little did they know what horror awaited them on the far side of the river. They may not have let Shelly out of their sights if they had.

An Enemy Lurks

"Alright, guys. Now, I don't know about you, but I haven't seen any flies yet, so I'm not quite sure which direction to go," Ribbit said.

"Hmm . . . well, according to my calculations, we have been heading east, and I always remember that the flies flew in to Lily Pad Hollow from the south. So, it makes sense that we head in that direction," Phinn estimated, holding his chin in thought and pointing downriver in the direction that Shelly had departed.

"Sounds good to me," Croak murmured.

"Yeah, me, too. Alright, Phinny boy, why don't you lead the way on this one?" Ribbit gently patted Phinn on his smooth, freckled back.

Thrilled to be put in charge, Phinn began leading them downriver, his eyes wide with excitement and his cheeks glowing with pride. They each held a reed in their hand and adventure in their hearts.

After wandering along the rocky riverbank for a few hours, they decided to stop and rest their aching legs. None of them had ever traveled so much in their lives and they were beginning to tire from lack of sleep.

Croak sat close to the water, casually plunking rocks into the river. Phinn refused to sit still and eagerly collected samples of plants and rocks, carefully placing them in his tiny containers. Ribbit scanned the area for some hint of where to go, but came up unsuccessful.

"Hey, guys. How about we call it a day?" Ribbit finally remarked, as he noticed the last rays of the sun smearing their way across the sky. Dusk was falling and the light was fading, a warning that soon it would be dark.

"Yeah, I need to sleep," Croak added.

"Good idea, boys. I think this area is probably the best one that we've seen along this bank so far." Phinn patted the spongy grass beneath him.

They decided to collect some supplies to make a tent for shelter for the night. Ribbit and Phinn grabbed whatever sticks they could find on the ground around them, while Croak hopped off into the trees, returning with some tall, sturdy leaves to use as covering.

Just as they put the finishing touches on their make-shift tent, there was a loud rumbling. Swollen gray clouds now prevailed, and within minutes, they burst open as rain poured from above.

Rain continued to fall for what seemed like hours. Ribbit, Croak, and Phinn huddled under their tent, listening to the pitter-patter of rain rolling off their leaf roof. When it got dark enough, Ribbit took out his firefly nightlight. It created a warm glow that reminded Ribbit of when they would make forts in his house and pretend that they were camping. He had to admit that the real thing was much more exhilarating!

Ribbit reached into his pack and took out one of his books by R.T. Hopkins. Reading had always comforted Ribbit in a way that nothing else could, and out of all the things he brought with him, this book was his most prized possession. It was the first book he had ever picked out on his own. R.T. Hopkins only made one copy of his books, since each was written by hand and bound by R.T. Hopkins himself, so it was a rare find in the used book store and it was more valuable to Ribbit than gold. Its hard cover was made of tree bark, but felt smooth and polished from years of use. Its bold lettering was etched into the wooden surface, revealing the title, *Salamander Sam,* just above the name of the all-important author himself: *R.T. Hopkins.* Ribbit had probably read this story a thousand times. It was about a salamander born with yellow spots, while all of his friends were spotless.

Ribbit wasn't sure why he liked this story so much. It probably had to do with the fact that Sam felt like he was different, the same way that Ribbit had always felt like he was different from the other frogs his age. Whatever the reason, this book held a special place for Ribbit and he would have never left it behind.

Now more than ever, Ribbit felt its words beckoning to him from their wrinkled pages, promising their familiarity in an unfamiliar place. He longed for its fantasy to carry him away from all of the fear and uncertainty he felt in this strange place. He figured Phinn and Croak could probably use an escape as well.

He crossed his legs and carefully opened the book as if he were opening a treasure chest containing all of the secrets of the world. He cleared his throat and began reading aloud to his companions, who lay in front of him on their stomachs, their hands resting under their chins and their big, eager eyes focused on Ribbit. He knew this story by heart, so he almost didn't need the text at all, but it was more fun to hold up the ancient book and read from its age-stained pages, the way it was meant to be read.

He tried his best to emulate how his father read to him each night, changing his tone for the different characters and drawing out the anticipation for what might happen next. He knew he couldn't tell a story as well as his father. His father could bring stories to life, taking words on a page and making them so relatable that you could feel the action and taste the intensity. If only Ribbit could do that now, his friends would forget about their troubles and be whisked away to another world.

Ribbit got so caught up in the story that he didn't even realize that Phinn and Croak had fallen asleep. *Had they heard the ending? That was the best part! Oh, well.* With a sigh, he carefully shut his book, placed it lovingly back in his pack, covered his firefly nightlight, laid on his back, and closed his eyes. The rain still fell

---

upon their leafy tent, sounding like fingers drumming to a wilderness beat.

This was the first night ever that Ribbit hadn't been tucked into bed by his parents. He could just imagine them saying, "Ribbit, I love you more than . . ." The memory brought tears to his eyes. He wondered if they were worried about him. He wondered how Zippy was doing now that he was gone. He felt guilty for leaving them without any explanations, but he knew that he had to go on this mission to save his town. They'll have to understand. *If I didn't do it, who would? It's for their own good*, he thought. With that determined thought in mind, he softly whispered good night to his parents, who seemed so far away, and drifted off to sleep to the sweet melody of the rain.

*****

The morning sunlight filtered through the cracks in the leaves, tickling Ribbit's face and rousing him from his slumber. Outside, birds chirped loudly as if calling him to get up and enjoy the day. He sat up, stretched his twiggy limbs and rubbed the drowsiness from his eyes. It took him a moment to get his bearings. He half expected to wake up in his own bed, hearing the clanging of his mother preparing breakfast and Zippy's singing filling the air, as if it were all a dream.

But it wasn't.

After a moment, Ribbit nudged his slumbering companions, urging them to wake up. He was met with moans and pleas for five more minutes. As he exited the tent, he could hear the gurgling of the swift-moving river. He breathed in the morning, letting it fill his lungs with its cool, crisp air. It was as if the rain had washed away all of his trouble and uncertainty, making the world refreshing and new. As he stretched out his aching legs, he began to wonder what the day had in store for them. After all, in one single day they had left Lily Pad Hollow, encountered a real-life turtle, crossed a rushing river, made a tent in the wilderness, and survived a rain storm in the wild, all of which were things that he never dreamed he would experience; at least, not in real life.

Not long after, Phinn and Croak got up and joined him beside the river. Croak began skipping stones on the water's surface, while Ribbit and Phinn sat quietly contemplating their next move.

"Guys, I was just thinking . . ." Phinn wandered off, cleaning his spectacles with a soft rag that he stuffed in his pocket. "The river goes on for quite a while. Maybe we should try to make another raft using the stuff we have for our tent and float our way downriver?"

Ribbit glanced at the tent, then back at Phinn. "Alright, I guess it's worth a shot." Then he turned to Croak, who clearly wasn't paying attention to their conversation. "Hey there, stone-thrower, you think you could try and take this tent apart to make it into a raft for us?"

"I guess," Croak nodded, throwing his last gray stone into the river with a final *kerplunk.*

Croak took apart the massive structure and they all worked together to construct their raft, using vines for rope and reeds for structure, until it was sturdy enough to carry them downriver.

"All aboard!" Croak shouted from the deck. The boys all jumped on and pushed off the riverbank, heading swiftly down the river to an unknown destination.

They made great time traveling with the current of the river, while also resting their weary legs and enjoying the opportunity to take in the scenery. All around them were colorful birds nestled high in the swaying trees, adding bright red, orange, and blue specks to the lush greenery. Schools of silver fish swam alongside their raft, their scales gleaming in the sunlight, while beautiful flying insects with colorful wings fluttered playfully in the air. Ribbit had never felt more alive. He longed to imprint in his mind what each new creature and plant looked liked. A wide-eyed Phinn was eagerly gathering as many samples as he could to add to his collection, while a seemingly unphased Croak steered the raft. Ribbit wished he had brought some paper along with them so that he could record all of his fascinating observations and add them to the famed stories of R.T. Hopkins. However, there was no time for such distractions. Although this experience was fantastic, it was not the real reason he was there. He was on a mission and he couldn't let the magic of it all distract him from that.

Just as this last thought left his mind, a great thump rattled the little raft.

"What was that?" Ribbit shrieked, looking over the edge of the raft and searching for a cause to that sizable jolt.

"I have no idea. Do you see anything?" Phinn called out, quickly gathering his samples and stuffing them into his pockets.

What a catastrophe it would be if any of them fell into the waters below. They would be hearing him moan about it for the rest of the trip, that was for sure.

"It sounded big." Croak peered over the edge of the raft as he tried to regain control of his steering.

Ribbit looked closely at the water below him. He could just make out a long, thin, brown, almost branch-like thing sticking out from under the raft.

"Uh oh! Hey, guys? I think that we may have hit a branch below us or something. It looks like we're dragging it with us," he said. But just as he finished that sentence, the branch underneath the raft began to move. It didn't move the way that he had expected a branch to move, stiff and inflexible. Instead, it flowed with the water, weaving from left to right in a graceful manner. *Sticks don't move that way.* Suddenly, he realized it was no stick at all.

"SNAKE!!!!" he screamed, hopping as far away from the edge of the raft as possible.

Croak and Phinn also hurtled themselves to the center of the raft and the three little frogs held each other tightly, bodies trembling and hearts racing, waiting for their worst nightmare to show itself.

After a moment of eerie silence, there was another great thump on the raft. The three frogs yelped with fear, and before they could catch their breath, the snake shot out of the crystal water and snapped its massive jaws at the frightened frogs, narrowly missing them before retreating back to the waters below.

"AHHH!" Phinn shouted. "This is it! This is it! Why did I let you talk me into this, Ribbit?"

"Pull yourself together, frog!" Croak demanded, slapping Phinn gently across the face to pull him to his senses.

"Ow! Okay, okay!" Phinn exclaimed. "I'm together! I'm together!" He rubbed his sore cheek and shot Croak an irritated look.

Ribbit wished that they had stayed on land—where they belonged—instead of floating helplessly along a river they knew nothing about. But this was no time to panic. Panicking would only make things worse. He simply had to deal with the situation they were in and try to figure out a way to get them out of it.

"Alright, guys. We have to come up with a plan. Do we still have those reeds handy for weapons?" Ribbit whispered, as if the snake could hear what they were saying from the deep water below.

Another thump rocked the raft. The boys squeezed together even tighter, wishing they could make themselves invisible.

"Yeah, over there!" Croak pointed toward the front end of the raft.

"Well, that's a lost hope. Anyone else got a plan?" Phinn scowled.

"What do you mean it's a lost hope?" Ribbit asked sharply.

"I mean, there is no way that we are getting all the way over there without getting eaten!" Phinn snarled with frustration.

"I'll get them if you guys can distract the snake and make him think that we're on the other side of the raft," Croak said confidently.

"Oh, alright Croak, and what kind of funeral service would you like us to provide for you when the snake eats you up? You want flowers or songs . . ." Phinn was really pushing it with his sarcasm.

"Cut it out, Phinn!" Ribbit gave up on whispering and was now yelling. "You got a better plan?"

Phinn stood there, motionless and silent.

"Didn't think so," Ribbit scoffed.

"Fine. And how do you suppose we go about doing this?" Phinn surrendered.

"How about you and I hop quickly toward the back end of the raft, making lots of noise, while Croak grabs the reeds from the front and we will meet back in the middle?" Ribbit felt proud of himself for coming up with an idea so quickly.

"Wow, that sounds like a terrible idea! So we're supposed to lure the snake to the back of the raft? What's to say that he won't just attack us there?" Phinn asked. He did have a point.

"It's a risk we're going to have to take. It's either that or we just sit here and wait to be eaten with no weapons to defend ourselves." Ribbit was getting upset with Phinn's pessimism when they were clearly in danger. "Are you in or out, Phinn?"

Phinn stood silent for a moment.

"In or out?" Ribbit repeated himself sternly.

Hesitantly, Phinn gave in. "Okay, okay. Fine, I'm in. Just tell me when to go."

"Croak, you ready?" Ribbit asked, as Croak nodded his head in approval. "Alright, on the count of three. One, two, three!"

Croak gave a giant leap toward the front of the raft, swooping up the reeds and returning to the center of the raft in the bat of an eye. At the same time, Ribbit and Phinn sprung toward the rear end of the raft, landing with a giant thud. Ribbit was pleasantly surprised that Phinn was able to pull off their plan since his jumping was usually so clumsy and uncoordinated.

As they expected, their thumping lured the snake. It burst out of the rushing water and sank its sharp fangs into the back of the raft. The massive jaws missed Phinn by an inch. He let out a high-pitched shriek of terror before he and Ribbit scrambled safely to the center of the raft.

After a moment of clinging to each other tightly and gasping for air, a relieved Ribbit called out, "Ah, ha! We've got them! Weapons gentlemen!"

Croak handed each of the frogs a reed and they clung to them tightly, bracing for the snake to attack again. They decided that the best plan of action was to stand at the center of the raft with their backs to each other, each frog pointing in a different direction, so that when the snake attacked again, one of them would see it and be able to stab it with their mighty reed.

Up ahead, two giant boulders blocked the rushing river, leaving an opening much too slender for the raft to squeeze through. There was no way for them to steer the raft away at this point, so all they could do was brace for impact. The raft came to an abrupt stop as it wedged tightly between the two boulders. They were stuck.

Without a moment to lose, the powerful snake rose from the water once more, snapping its fierce jaws at the three trembling frogs. They stabbed recklessly in the air, attempting to ward off the predator. Croak sunk a few good jabs into the snake's belly and let out a victorious cry. However, his celebration was cut short as the jabs appeared to merely slow the snake down—not cause him any real pain. What else could they do? They had to just keep jabbing him until the discomfort made him retreat—or so they hoped.

As the battle wore on, Ribbit bounded around the raft until he suddenly found himself cornered. There was nowhere to run. If he hopped forward he was hopping directly into the mouth of the snake. Bad idea. If he hopped backward or to either side, he would fall into the water, which was the snake's territory and would definitely mean certain death. Bad idea. He had to accept the inevitable and try to put up a good fight.

Ribbit held out his reed and winced in terror, awaiting his fate. As the ferocious snake arched his back to strike, he suddenly turned his attention away from Ribbit toward the water. His body jostled and jerked from something under the water. He began writhing around, his eyes scanning the glassy surface for the invisible enemy, when a mighty force gave his tail a powerful yank. As quickly as the snake had shot out of the water for his attack, he was pulled back into the water far below. All that remained on the surface were the bubbles of where the snake used to be.

Ribbit, Croak, and Phinn stood motionless for a moment, until they were sure that the coast was clear. Then Ribbit very cautiously tiptoed to the edge of the raft and looked directly down into the clear water. His face lit up with excitement.

"Guys, you gotta see this!" He exclaimed, waving for his friends to come over.

"No, I'm good over here in the center of the raft where it's safe," Phinn squealed.

"Oh, come on, Phinny boy! You're gonna want to see this!" Ribbit cried out once more, a smile overtaking his face.

Phinn and Croak cautiously hopped over and their mouths dropped in amazement. Below the raft, two turtles were wrapping the giant snake tightly around a boulder using long, sturdy vines. They used their hard, unforgiving shells as armor to deflect the snake's bites as they continued to wrap him tightly around the boulder until he could move no more.

The three frogs began hooting and hollering aboard their raft, dancing and slapping high fives in celebration of their victory. They had actually battled a snake and lived to tell the tale! No one in Lily Pad Hollow would ever believe this!

Once the snake was secured tightly to the rock, the turtles left it behind and swam up to the raft.

"Are you frogs okay?" the larger turtle asked. Then she boarded the raft with the smaller turtle that Ribbit immediately recognized to be Shelly.

"Yeah, we're fine. Thanks for saving us!" Ribbit exclaimed, hopping over to greet his new friends.

"I knew it wouldn't be the last I saw of you crazy froggies," Shelly giggled as the three frogs pounced on her, engulfing her in hugs.

"How did you know we were in trouble?" Ribbit asked, still squeezing his friend tightly, afraid that if he let go she would leave.

"My mom and I were by the river bank over there and we heard a girl screaming."

"Oh, that was no girl. That was Phinn!" Croak blurted. They all roared with laughter.

Phinn blushed as he crossed his arms and turned his head in the opposite direction, his cheeks rosy with embarrassment. "Well excuse me for not making a more manly noise as I was dodging a giant evil snake who was trying to eat me!" he remarked sourly.

"Oh, it's alright Phinn. I'm just glad that you're all okay, even if you do scream like a girl," Shelly said, scooping Phinn up with her stubby hands and placing him on top of her beautiful shell. "This is my mom, Myrtle. She's the real reason that you froggies are safe."

"Oh, Shelly knows I couldn't have done it without her. That darn snake has been bothering critters in this area for far too long and it was time to teach him a lesson. It'll be a long while before he's able to make his way out of the bindings we put him in, so hopefully he'll think twice before terrorizing helpless frogs like you again." Her eyes twinkled as she spoke. "Now, I insist that ya'll stay with us for the evening. We live just on the other side of that hill downriver."

"Wow, that would be great. I think that we could use a little down time after that run-in." Ribbit gave Myrtle a big hug. It felt nice to have the warmth and comfort of being close to a mother again. And with that, the two turtles and three little frogs headed toward the turtles' home nestled in a grassy knoll nearby. The boys were looking forward to a restful evening, feeling safer and more welcomed than they had felt since they left Lily Pad Hollow.

An Evening at the Turtle Home

Shelly and Myrtle's home was very quaint and reminded Ribbit a lot of his own. He hadn't realized until that very moment how much he longed for the smell and feel of home. It was filled with all sorts of token objects, like a shiny snail shell, a beautiful purple crystal, a piece of wood that resembled the shape of a turtle, and a small fossil of a skeletal fish. All of these treasures were placed neatly on wooden shelves that lined the walls of the living room. In between the wooden shelves were many pictures of the Turtle family. There was one of them swimming together, splashing happily in the warm, summer sun. Another was of a much younger Shelly staring intently at a grasshopper with a look of wonder on her face. Ribbit guessed that it was probably her first encounter with the little critter. Another one pictured the whole family (including Mr. Turtle, whom Ribbit hadn't met yet) standing in front of their cozy, little home. Lastly, there was a very old picture of Myrtle smiling with a look of nervousness and excitement as she cradled a small, white egg beneath her belly. Ribbit instantly loved the feeling of being in the Turtle household. It felt just like home.

As soon as she entered the house, Myrtle headed straight for the kitchen to prepare a meal for her new guests. Croak followed closely behind and watched in awe as she took out five slimy slugs for supper. He had never seen anyone prepare a slug to eat before. He couldn't take his eyes off her as she rubbed the slick skin of the slugs with seasonings, such as duckweed and algae, and threw the slugs onto a sizzling frying pan. His mouth watered at the aroma of the delicious new entrée. He was going to like it here.

Phinn, on the other hand, was less worried about the new cuisine they were about to eat and more interested in learning everything he could about Shelly. Since they left the river bank, Phinn had bombarded Shelly with a million questions like, "What is it like to be a turtle?" "How many times have you seen snakes?" and "Does it hurt to wear a hard shell on your back?" Shelly answered all of his answers in a short, curt tone, sending a distinct message that she was getting annoyed with all of his queries. Phinn was either unaware of her annoyance or was choosing to ignore it because he kept on interrogating her.

When it was finally time to eat, Shelly sat in between Ribbit and Croak, so Phinn couldn't ask her any more questions. Ribbit stared at the slippery slug that Myrtle plopped with a *splat* on the plate in front of him. He was wondering if he would be able to stomach such a strange supper.

"I hope you enjoy it, my little froggy friends! It's a secret recipe that has been passed down in the Turtle family for generations," Myrtle said, as she served herself the last slimy slug and took a seat at the head of the table.

Shelly quickly slid her slug into her mouth and blurted, "Eat up, guys. This grub is good!"

Croak was the first of the frogs to slurp up his slug. Phinn and Ribbit watched his reaction closely, gauging whether it was edible or not. There were few things Ribbit hated more than throwing up, so he wasn't taking any chances. When Croak looked pleased and continued chewing his food without spitting any of it out, Phinn and Ribbit decided it was safe. They both gulped down their slugs and were surprised at how much they enjoyed this new food that, until today, they never would have imagined they would eat.

"Wait until I tell Speckles about this. Her fly-eating victory will be nothing against us eating slugs for dinner!" Croak exclaimed, holding his full belly in delight.

"Oh, and Kilroy and Squiggy will never believe that we fought off . . ." Phinn stopped abruptly, glanced over at Shelly and Myrtle, cleared his throat, and corrected himself. "Uh, I mean, YOU guys fought off a snake that was about to eat us! They'll keel over and die when they hear that!" Phinn shrieked with excitement.

"Not sure who those Kilroy and Squiggy frogs are, but by the way y'all are talking, I'm guessing they deserve whatever is coming to them. So, in that case, we are glad to be of service," Myrtle announced, flashing the boys a proud smile.

"Why are you froggies here anyway?" Shelly blurted out. "You run away or something?"

"Yeah, I guess," Ribbit shrugged. He hadn't really looked at it that way before. "But it's not like we're mad at our parents or anything. We're on a mission to find out why flies and mosquitoes have stopped coming to our town. That's pretty much all that we eat and so it's kinda important we find out what's going on."

"Wow. Bummer," Shelly murmured, her mouth full of food.

"Hmmm . . . that's peculiar. We've had that problem around these parts recently, too. Many of our friends and neighbors have suffered without the flies and mosquitoes that usually travel through here. Lucky for us, my husband, Otis, must know of a fantastic spot to find flies because he has been returning home with pods full of them for the last few weeks. We have one out back right now, in fact."

"Really!" Ribbit's heart raced. "Do you happen to know where he's getting them?"

"No, sorry dear. Unfortunately, I don't know and Otis is out of town until the end of the week. If you wish to stay, you may ask him when he returns."

Disappointment weighed on Ribbit's heart. His face felt so heavy he couldn't even fake a smile. He wasn't going to get the answers he sought for here. "Unfortunately, we can't stay that long," he sighed.

"Well, I'm sorry I couldn't be more help," Myrtle responded sadly staring at her empty, slimy plate. "But what I can offer you is a nice warm fly scramble breakfast tomorrow morning."

Ribbit didn't want Myrtle to feel badly about not being able to help him. She had already done so much (including saving his life) and the last thing he wanted to do was make her feel bad. So he put on a big smile for her. "Wow! A fly breakfast would be great!" he exclaimed. "And the slugs were delicious, Mrs. Turtle. We insist on cleaning up."

Phinn and Croak shot him a disgruntled look. Ribbit gave them both a gentle kick under the table and stared at them with wide, serious eyes.

"Uh, yeah. We'd like to help you clean up and stuff," Croak muttered under his breath as he rubbed his now aching foot.

"Yeah, sure," Phinn added with a fake grin plastered across his face.

"Well what a nice little treat! Thank you," Myrtle tilted her head in gratitude. "It certainly is nice to have someone else volunteer to clean up around here." She raised her eyebrows, giving Shelly a look that spoke mountains.

"Hey, don't look at me! I was out there saving them too and I'm gonna take me a nice little break," Shelly sassed. "Thanks, froggies!" She shouted as she headed toward the living room.

Once the two turtles were in the other room and out of earshot, Phinn jabbed Ribbit in the ribs with his elbow and muttered, "Great. What'd you do that for?"

"Hey, they saved our lives. The least we can do is the dishes, guys!" Ribbit insisted, as he cleared the table and began rinsing off the slimy plates. Phinn and Croak shared a tired, unhappy look, but didn't say a word of rebuttal. They knew Ribbit was right, so they helped him clean up the dishes and make some hibiscus tea for them all to enjoy.

"Can you believe how close we were to finding a clue about where the flies are going? If only Mr. Turtle were here," Ribbit whispered, so as not to have Shelly and Mrs. Turtle overhear.

"I know! I was freaking out when she said that Mr. Turtle was bringing home pods filled with flies," Phinn whispered back as he poured some piping hot tea into a small teacup made from the shell of a snail. Seeing the familiar shell reminded Ribbit of Smudge. It sent a chill down his spine to think that he would be drinking from the shell of a mollusk like his favorite pet. Although Ribbit had read of frogs and many other animals eating snails, the frogs of Lily Pad Hollow never ate them; it was like eating their pets, which just didn't seem right. However, he didn't want to offend his new friends' customs, so he decided to put his feelings aside and drink from the teacups, regardless of how gross and unusual it seemed to him.

"I wonder where Mr. Turtle is," Croak added, though not in such a quiet whisper as his friends.

"I have no idea. Do you think it would be weird if I asked them where he is?" Ribbit whispered back as he prepared a tray to put the snail shell teacups on.

"I suppose it really is none of our business, but it couldn't hurt to ask. I was wondering the same thing myself," Phinn shruged, spilling some of his tea onto the counter. They all shared a giggle at Phinn's clumsiness as they cleaned up the spilled tea and refilled the teacup. "Hey, you think they would let me take home one of their trinkets as a sample? Maybe the purple stone or the wooden turtle?"

"No, Phinn! Besides, you can't go around asking people if you can take their stuff. It's rude," Ribbit whispered sharply.

"Fine, fine, fine. I just figured it was worth a shot." Phinn rolled his eyes.

After the kitchen was spotless, the three frogs joined their new friends in the living room to enjoy some tea by the fire and share stories of their lives. Ribbit began by telling Shelly and Myrtle more about their mission to return the flies to Lily Pad Hollow, which they agreed was a noble task indeed. Then, the Turtles shared stories about their lives. Turns out, Shelly had had a very different life than anything Ribbit could have imagined. The Turtle family had traveled to different lands, eaten far away cuisines, and had friends that ranged from a small bird that Shelly called a *swallow* to a fish called a *river trout*. Quite a different life from the sheltered one that Ribbit had led in Lily Pad Hollow. He sat there quietly trying to absorb as many details as he could remember so he could share all of the fascinating specifics with his family when he got home.

After Shelly finished telling a story about their family camping trip upriver, Ribbit saw an opportunity for the question he

91

was dying to ask. "Um, not to be too forward and feel free not to answer this, but where is Mr. Turtle?"

"How silly of me. I told you that he was out of town and failed to fill in all the details. I must really be losing it!" Myrtle's eyes rolled up toward the ceiling and she tapped the side of her head with her stubby hand. "Otis is traveling upriver to visit some of our family. We're expecting him back later this week. I decided to stay here with Shelly because she can't miss any school. School is much too important and we'll visit our family during Shelly's break."

"You mean you go to school, too, Shelly?" Phinn exclaimed gleefully. He loved school and delighted at any opportunity to discuss it.

"Of course I go to school. I am no dumb-dumb. School is awesome! I'm in the coolest class right now where we're learning all about biology."

"What's biology?" Croak was the only one brave enough to ask, even though Ribbit and Phinn had no clue what biology was either.

"Oh, it's so cool! You learn about all the different kinds of plants and animals that live around here. You get to go on field trips and we even get to try eating different plants and bugs and stuff. It's totally my favorite subject." Shelly's face lit up as she described what her school was like. "The best part is that my best friend Broxton gets to sit right next to me."

"Oh, Shelly and that badger are inseparable!" Myrtle shook her head playfully.

"Whoa! You go to school with badgers?" Phinn could hardly contain his excitement and he nearly spilled his tea all over himself.

"Yeah! Badgers, squirrels, all different kinds of birds, you name it! In fact, I'm the only turtle in my class."

"Wow! That's amazing!" Ribbit couldn't help but feel envious. Dragonfly Elementary seemed so boring compared to Shelly's school. For a moment, Ribbit daydreamed what it would be like to go to school with Shelly and learn about biology and be in class with different animals. It just sounded like so much more fun than learning how to catch flies with a bunch of plain ol' frogs.

Myrtle glanced at the clock. "Oh, dear! It's getting late. I think it's best that we all be off to bed. Let me show you froggies where you will be sleeping for the night." As she got up to escort the boys to the guest bedroom down the hall, she called out to Shelly. "Shelly, would you be a dear and put all of the tea cups in the kitchen for me before you head to bed?"

Ribbit's heart stopped. He couldn't believe what he was hearing. Did she really just say "would you be a dear?" or was he just missing his mother so much that he was beginning to imagine things? After a moment's pause, he decided that he, in fact, was not hearing things and he was more convinced than ever that Myrtle was just the motherly figure he needed right now.

"Ugh, fine," Shelly sighed, as she began gathering all the teacups. "Night, froggies!"

The boys trailed after Myrtle as she led them into the guest room. Inside there was a bunk bed, a giant overstuffed couch, and a small wooden desk. The beds were covered in brown patchwork quilts that looked cozy and inviting. On the far wall there was a small round window that offered the most amazing view of the river. Ribbit leapt over to the window and took a moment to gaze out through the circular glass, watching the busy river rush by rapidly. He found it fascinating that the river would continue to be hard at work, tirelessly plowing through the land, while the rest of the world was sleeping.

"I hope this room is to your liking," Myrtle said. Croak promptly bumped Phinn out of his way and called dibs on the top bunk, while a scowl-faced Phinn resigned himself to the bottom.

"This is wonderful, Mrs. Turtle," Ribbit responded. "Thank you very much for all you've done for us. We really appreciate it. Really."

"It's been my pleasure," Myrtle grinned as she slowly began to shut the door. "Now try and get some sleep. See you in the morning."

"Good night!" Phinn called out.

"Good night, Mrs. T!" Croak added, fluffing up his pillow and wriggling comfortably in his new bed.

"Good night," Ribbit echoed, as he turned back toward the window to stare out into the world. He began to think about all that had happened since they had left Lily Pad Hollow. It was so amazing to think that while all of the other frogs in Lily Pad Hollow were doing the same old things and sleeping in the same old rooms, he was staying the night with turtles.

"What are you doing, Rib?" Phinn asked, already nestled in his bed.

"Oh, nothing. Just looking outside," Ribbit responded casually.

"Well, come on then. Let's get to bed already!" Croak hollered from the top bunk. He looked very snug with his round face peeking out from the comfy patchwork quilt.

"Alright, alright. Good night guys," Ribbit said as he crept onto his bed.

"Night!" said Phinn.

"Don't let the bed bugs bite. Or if they do, just send them my way. Those guys are delicious!" Croak chuckled. The boys all gave a little giggle, then the room fell silent.

Ribbit slid into the crisp sheets of his bed, snuggled up under the warm covers, and rested his head on his spongy pillow. He could hear the faint sound of the bustling river lapping on the rocky shore as he drifted off to sleep.

Do You See What I See?

The bright morning light peered through the circular window of the guest room, stirring the frogs from their slumber. They had been so exhausted from their journey that they had managed to do some crazy things in their sleep. Croak had tightly wrapped himself up like a burrito in his patchwork quilt. His mouth was opened wide and he was snoring so loudly that it sounded as if a wild pig were in his bed. Phinn, on the other hand, had kicked off all of his covers and had somehow managed to turn completely around so that his head was at the foot of the bed and his feet were on his pillow. Beside his face sat a puddle of drool, which made a dark spot on the brown sheet. Ribbit's bed, on the other hand, was empty as he lay snoozing soundly on the floor. He had fallen off his bed during the night without even waking.

Croak was the first one up, so he decided to use his throwing talents to launch his pillow at Phinn and Ribbit to wake them up as well. Once the boys had gotten themselves together and cleaned themselves up a bit, they opened the door to the guest room and headed toward the kitchen to eat breakfast with Shelly and Myrtle.

Ribbit devoured his fly scramble breakfast leaving no leg, wing, or thorax uneaten. The familiar flavor warmed both his stomach and his heart. For a moment, he closed his eyes and was back in Lily Pad Hollow: sitting at his kitchen table, his mother in front of the stove, humming her familiar tune, Zippy singing along, and the sound of his father's hammer tinkering in the background.

A loud knocking sound abruptly brought Ribbit back to reality, back to the Turtle home, back to his same predicament.

"Now, who could that be? We weren't expecting any visitors." Myrtle set her napkin on her plate. "Ya'll just enjoy your breakfast and I'll be right back."

Ribbit, Phinn, and Croak exchanged quiet glances as Myrtle stood up and headed toward the door. They strained their ears to hear who the mystery guest was. The deep tone suggested that it was a male. Maybe it was someone who knew something about the flies?

As if they all had the same thought, the three frogs quickly leapt out of their seats and headed toward the door, leaving Shelly in the kitchen, still stuffing her face with fly scramble.

"Why, hello there," the animal greeted the boys as they crowded in the doorway. Ribbit didn't even have to ask, for he knew right away that it was a lizard. He was very handsome, with big, glossy eyes and textured skin that looked like tiny, colored beads. He was exactly what Ribbit imagined a lizard would look like—clean cut and very polished. "Who are these young fellas?" he asked, flashing a charming grin.

"Oh, this is Ribbit, Croak, and Phinn. They are staying with us for a little while," Myrtle announced. "And boys, this is Alexander. He's a friend of the family; we've known him for . . . how long would you say, Alexander? Three, maybe four years?"

"Oh, Myrtle. Time does fly. I actually believe I have had the pleasure of your friendship for going on five years now."

"Has it been that long? I must be getting old," Myrtle chuckled.

"Oh, you look exactly the same as the day I met you, Myrtle. And I'm not just saying that because you make the best grilled slugs in town," Alexander smiled, giving Ribbit a wink.

"Oh, you flatter me so. It's a lie, but I'll take it," Myrtle blushed.

"So, what brings you little frogs to the river?" Alexander grinned, his white teeth gleaming.

"Oh, it's a fascinating story!" Myrtle interrupted. "They are looking for the missing flies. You know how difficult things have been for the folks who have been without them for so long. So, these young fellas are on a mission to return the flies."

Alexander's face twisted at Myrtle's remarks. "Well, that's quite a pursuit you are on, little frogs. I hope you know what you are getting yourselves into. I mean, the world can be a very dangerous place. Have you ever travelled before?" he asked, staring intently at the boys.

"No, sir, we haven't," Ribbit said. Croak and Phinn shook their heads no.

"There are some really bad guys out there, you know. Predators capable of things you can't even imagine. Have you frogs thought about that?"

"Yes, sir. We have." Croak and Phinn nodded in agreement.

"And it's just the three of you? No adults?"

"Yes, sir, it is." Ribbit answered again. He could feel the doubt radiating from Alexander. This is exactly why he didn't want to tell anyone about his plans. He wanted to avoid moments like this.

"You seem like nice boys and as noble as your intentions are, I think you best be on your way back home. Let the adults handle this one. The world out there is no place for three young frogs. I do believe you are in over your heads with this one, boys. Don't you agree, Myrtle?" No words could have irritated Ribbit more.

"Actually, while it's very sweet of you to worry, Alexander, I'd have to disagree. Maybe we need some young eyes on the situation. It appears we adults haven't been able to come up with any answers on our own. Sometimes it takes a fresh eye to see something that was right in front of us and I think these three frogs might be just the thing we need." She proudly wrapped her arm around the boys and tapped them gently on the back.

"If you say so, Myrtle. I'd just hate to see anyone get hurt, that's all," Alexander shrugged. He looked at Ribbit and could see his words had frustrated him. "Didn't meant to overstep my boundaries here and I do apologize if I offended you in any way. Just ignore me. I don't even know what I'm talking about, really. In fact, I think what you are doing is very brave. I'd offer to help you little frogs out, but, unfortunately, duty calls and I must tend to my business."

Myrtle quickly changed the subject. "Alexander here tends to the amazing herb garden. He owns his own shop in town and I wouldn't cook using anything else." Myrtle smiled warmly. "So, my dear friend, what brings you to our home today?"

"Ah, yes, I brought you some fresh duckweed." He pulled the fragrant herbs from his satchel and handed them to Myrtle.

"Why, thank you, Alexander. That was very thoughtful. Tell me you didn't come all this way just to bring this for us? I could have come to your store to pick it up."

"Actually, I was wondering if I could have a word with that strapping husband of yours. Is he in?" Alexander asked, removing his brown hat from his head.

"Unfortunately, he's not. Otis is visiting some family upriver. Would you like me to tell him that you came by when he returns?"

"Umm . . . that won't be necessary, Myrtle." He gave an edgy grin. "I'll just catch up with him when he returns. Exactly, when are you expecting him back?"

"At the end of the week. Are you sure you don't want me to pass a message along?" Myrtle asked. "It would be no problem."

"Oh, no. Really, it's no big deal," Alexander quickly interrupted. "As I said, I'll just catch up with him when he returns then." He placed his worn brown hat back on beaded head. "Have a great day, Myrtle. So sorry to interrupt your morning."

"Come back anytime, Alexander," Myrtle smiled warmly. "And thanks for the duckweed. I was just starting to run low."

"It was nice to meet you, Ribbit, Phinn, and Croak. I hope you find what you are looking for." With one last look, Alexander turned around and strolled away.

Myrtle breathed in the aroma from her handful of herbs as she turned around and began to walk back into the kitchen. Ribbit, Croak, and Phinn stayed at the door, watching Alexander disappear from sight.

"Alright, little ones. Why don't you head outside and play for a while? After what happened yesterday, I'm sure you could use a little fun," Myrtle called out from the kitchen.

The boys thought about it for a moment, then agreed that one hour of playtime couldn't hurt, so they all headed outside to run and frolic. Shelly taught them how to play new games, like Jump-a-roo and Skippy Freeze. They were having such a good time that they completely forgot about their mission - for the moment, at least.

After Phinn was declared the winner of Skippy Freeze, they all plopped to the ground in a massive heap. Phinn let out a triumphant cry and began to laugh hysterically at his win. He had played the game surprisingly well for a frog that didn't have an athletic bone in his body. It probably had to do with the logic involved in the game. Logic was always Phinn's thing and it irked Croak that Phinn had beat him in a physical game for the first time ever.

For a few moments, they all just laid there, the grass tickling their arms and legs, staring up at the sky. Shelly broke the silence when she turned to the frogs and asked in a secretive tone, "Hey froggies, wanna see something cool?"

"Of course we do!" Ribbit sat up excitedly.

"Uh-huh," Croak wheezed, holding his gut. He was the last person to be "it", so he was still trying to catch his breath.

"Oh, what is it?" Phinn asked. He was still glowing from his victory.

"I asked if you wanted to see something cool, not hear something cool, Phinn. I have to show you. Follow me!" Shelly said as she shot up and began to walk away. The boys quickly followed.

Shelly took the boys to the edge of the river, where a fallen tree had made a bridge. The four of them balanced carefully across the log. Once on the other side of the river, Shelly led the boys to the trunk of a tree that had a large hole as an entrance. Next to the hole was a crudely written sign that read, "Shelly and Broxton's Fort."

"Welcome to my fort, froggies!" Shelly exclaimed proudly as she ducked into the opening, disappearing inside the darkness of the massive tree. The three frogs followed her in and immediately found themselves steeped in darkness, unable to see their hands in front of their faces. The blackness suddenly lit up as Shelly flicked a jar with a glow-worm in it, similar to the firefly nightlights the frogs of the

Hollow used. They squinted at the light until their eyes adjusted. The room glowed an eerie green color, just bright enough for them to see each other's faces and to notice all of the books and trinkets that decorated the wooden walls.

"Whoa . . . cool hangout!" Croak shouted excitedly.

"Yeah, this place is awesome!" Ribbit exclaimed, taking a moment to circle the entire room.

"I wish we had a place like this at home!" Phinn said, admiring a drawing that Shelly had done of her and Broxton playing in the river.

"This is where I escape to read books, make up stories, and draw pictures with Broxton. But it's totally a secret, so you froggies can't tell anyone about it."

"Our lips are sealed," Ribbit assured her. He returned to his snooping, when his eye was caught by a book as blue as a patch of sky. He promptly picked it up and began reading. It was titled *Sparrow's Journey Home*. How wonderful it was to read a new book about different animals than the ones he was used to reading about.

"You like that book, Ribbit?" Shelly asked, as she plopped down next to Ribbit on the dirt floor.

"Yeah, we don't have any books about sparrows at home." He caressed the book lovingly with his fingers, feeling the smooth binding and letting his fingers trace every letter on its cover.

"Really? Then why don't you keep it?" Shelly shrugged.

Ribbit's heart beat faster. *Was she serious?*

"Oh, no. I couldn't. It's your book, Shelly." Ribbit's parents had taught him that he was supposed to say that when someone offered him something valuable.

"No, I insist. I've read that book a million times and am kinda sick of it."

"Are you sure?" He had to ask one more time, even though he was dying to accept her offer.

"Yes, already! Take it!" Shelly put the book in Ribbit's hands. "Seriously, don't make me answer you again!" she sassed.

"Alright, alright!" Ribbit giggled. "Thanks, Shelly. I promise I'll take good care of it."

"Whatever," she smiled and gave him a playful wink.

After exploring Shelly's fort for about an hour, they all decided it was time to head back and get something to eat for lunch. As they crossed the fallen tree, Ribbit's attention was unexpectedly drawn upward as he heard a familiar buzzing sound.

"Ooh! Ooh! Ooh!" Ribbit cried, pointing up at the sky. "Flies! I see flies! We have to follow them, guys!" Ribbit shouted. "Shelly, can you get us back to your house quickly. We have to get our things and follow those flies!"

"Way ahead of you!" And with that, Shelly hurried the frogs back to her grassy knoll home. The boys swiftly gathered their belongings, gave Shelly and Myrtle many hugs and thanks, then headed out to follow the flies. If only they had been more careful to look where they were going.

Danger Up Ahead

Ribbit could feel his mouth watering as he frantically hurdled through the air, trying to catch those rascally insects he was so fond of. A few times, he got close to catching one; however, his attempts failed miserably and his tongue repeatedly came whizzing back into his mouth without a fly.

Phinn stumbled along beside his friends, tripping over his own webbed feet. His tongue zapped left and right, up and down . . . all over the place! But not in the right place.

Croak flung his pink, gluey tongue at a fly that had wandered from its swarm. At the exact moment that his tongue snapped forward, the fly zigged when he zagged and darted away. In his efforts, Croak not only missed his target, but also had somehow managed to wind his tongue tightly around a tree branch, leaving him tongue-tied. He tugged and tugged at his wound-up tongue, but was getting nowhere on his own.

In his leaping frenzy, Ribbit noticed that his friend was in quite a pickle, so he stopped his fly-hunting and turned around to help a desperate Croak pull his tongue from the branch.

Phinn, on the other hand, completely oblivious to Croak's predicament, kept on skittering after his prey. In fact, he was so intent on catching those flies, that his glasses flew off of his face and he didn't even stop to retrieve them. He just kept leaping almost as blind as a bat, chasing flies that seemed to be teasing him, flying just out of his reach.

Ribbit tried this way and that to unwrap Croak's tongue from the branch, but it was no use. "What in pond scum did you do here? Ugh . . ." Ribbit said as he took hold of Croak's sticky tongue and tugged it upward.

"OWWWW!" Croak moaned, his tongue still just as tangled as ever.

"Oops! Sorry, Croak," Ribbit said sympathetically. "Let's just try taking the end and looping it back through." Ribbit carefully unraveled Croak's snarled tongue from the branch.

Once he was finally freed, a relieved Croak thanked Ribbit and rubbed his sore tongue. Just then, Ribbit looked around. For the first time, the woods they were just leaping and bounding through happily seemed a lot scarier than he had thought. He hadn't noticed that they had jumped into a place darkened by tall, crooked trees, with a gray foggy mist creeping along the forest floor.

"Hey, where's Phinny boy?" Ribbit asked Croak, who simply shrugged in response. "Phinn!" he shouted. They listened carefully, expecting to hear Phinn's response or at least a high-pitched squeal in the distance. However, they were met with only the sound of birds chirping and the distant gurgling of the river behind them. "Hey Phinny boy! Where are you?" Ribbit called out again, still receiving no response.

After scanning the area for their missing friend, Croak shook his head. "I don't think he's here, Ribbit."

"We gotta go look for him," Ribbit said frantically.

"What if we split up to cover more ground? I'll go this way . . ." Croak pointed to the right. "And you go that way." He pointed to the left.

Ribbit rolled his eyes. "Yeah, that's a good idea," he snapped sarcastically. "Then we'll *all* be lost out here. There's no way we're splitting up!"

Croak's eyes fell down to the floor and he began kicking the dirt in embarrassment. "Okay, okay. Maybe it was a bad idea."

As soon as the words had left Ribbit's mouth, he felt guilty. "Sorry, Croak. That was real lousy of me. I'm just worried that's all. And I really don't want to lose you, too. Forgive me?"

"Yep," Croak said, giving Ribbit a little smile assuring him that all was forgiven. "You were right. We shouldn't split—" Before Croak could finish his sentence, the boys heard a high-pitched shrieking coming from the murky woods. It sounded as if it was straight ahead of them, but it was hard to tell. The fog filled the air with its twisty gray arms, clouding their vision and making it impossible to see more than a few feet ahead.

"I'd know that shriek anywhere!" Ribbit called out anxiously.

"Phinn!" the boys hollered, leaping furiously through the fog, into the direction of all the noise. The echoes of the distant birds and the sound of the rushing river died and the world went silent as they bounded aimlessly through the trees. The forest was a dark, tangled maze that seemingly had no end. How were they ever going to find Phinn in this mess?

"Help! Help! AHHHHH!" Phinn wailed, shattering the silence. Ribbit and Croak followed the direction of his cries until they came to a sudden halt. Before them was the sharp edge of a tall cliff. Since they had picked up so much speed from leaping, Croak had to quickly grab Ribbit by the arm and, using all of his strength, hold Ribbit back from tumbling off the edge.

"Whew! That was a close one. Thanks, Croak," Ribbit panted as he held on to his chest to keep his heart from jumping out.

"No prob," Croak responded, equally as out of breath from fear and exhaustion.

"AHH! GUYS! DOWN HERE, DOWN HERE!!!" Phinn shrieked. Ribbit and Croak heard him loud and clear, so they knew they were close.

"Where? Where are you?" Ribbit called out urgently, looking everywhere along the edge of the cliff.

"DOWN HERE!! DOWN HERE! DOOOOOWWWWNNN HEEERRRREEE!" Phinn wailed loudly.

Ribbit and Croak were sure now where Phinn's voice was coming from, although they both didn't want to admit it.

They took a long, deep breath before they got on their hands and knees and leaned over the edge of the cliff. As they looked down through the fog, they could make out the outline of Phinn's familiar face. He was hanging desperately on to a root, his legs flailing and his eyes as large as saucers.

"Leaping lily pads, am I glad to see you guys!" A grin flickered across his face as his hands strained to hold on to the wiry root.

"Phinn! How did this happen?" Ribbit asked.

"I was chasing the flies and my glasses fell off—" He stopped mid-sentence as the root began to loosen from its rocky base and his body lurched downward. "JUST PULL ME UP! PULL ME UP!" he screamed.

"Okay! Croak, reach down and see if you can grab ahold of Phinn's hand," Ribbit instructed. Croak laid down on his belly and reached his arm down to a frantic Phinn, stretching as long as he could. It was no use. He just couldn't reach him.

"Let me try! Let me try!" Ribbit demanded. He laid on his belly beside Croak and reached out to a dangling Phinn. Ribbit's arms were a bit longer than Croak's and he managed to grab onto Phinn.

"Gotcha!" Ribbit cried, trying to keep a strong hold on Phinn's slippery wrist. "Okay, when I count to three, Croak, I want you to pull me from behind. Phinn, I want you to let go of the root and we will fling you back up to land here. Got it?"

"Yep!" Croak acknowledged loudly, as he sprung to his feet and wrapped his arms around Ribbit's body.

"Okay," whimpered Phinn, a desperate look piercing his eyes.

"Alright." Ribbit swallowed a big gulp, heaved a deep sigh, and counted. "One, two, THREE!" He felt his whole body jostle as Croak used all of his strength to pull his body up. He also felt all of Phinn's weight, which was now as heavy as ten frogs, tugging on his arm, as Phinn let go of the crumbling root and dangled from Ribbit's grip.

Phinn whimpered and sucked in a deep breath, his wide eyes staring intensely into Ribbit's, as if begging him not to let him go. His feet clawed desperately along the rocky cliff, seeking a ledge or something to cling on to. Suddenly, his grip began to loosen. *No! No! Don't let him slip!* Ribbit's mind screamed as he tried with all of his might to tighten his hold.

His hand throbbed as he squeezed Phinn's wrist with every last ounce of energy he had. His grab was gradually loosening on Phinn and there was nothing he could do to stop it. Try as he might, Phinn was still slipping.

Staring eye to eye with his best buddy, Ribbit's heart came to a standstill. As if in slow motion, Phinn's wrist slid from his fingers.

Phinn's bloodcurdling screams echoed in the air. Ribbit stopped breathing and he watched his wailing friend fall away from him and disappear into the fog. His arm was still outstretched, reaching for Phinn, who was no longer there. All that remained was the fog. He couldn't stand to watch anymore, so he clenched his eyes shut. He no longer felt Phinn's weight tugging on his arm. He no longer felt Phinn's slippery skin on his fingers. He no longer heard Phinn gasping for air. He no longer felt anything. Phinn was gone.

Their Darkest Hour

Ribbit and Croak had never felt such grief, such sorrow, such sadness. Ribbit thought that he had felt true sadness before when his first pet snail ran (or slid rather) away from home. Ribbit thought that was going to be the worst that he would ever feel. Boy, he couldn't have been more wrong. This was so much worse.

The two friends sat on the edge of the cliff, staring blankly out into the fog, lost in thought for what seemed like hours. Finally, Croak broke the silence.

"It's not your fault, Ribbit. It's not anyone's fault," he said gloomily. He couldn't look Ribbit in the eye; he knew it would be too overwhelming for both of them.

Ribbit didn't respond. He just continued to stare blankly out into the nothingness ahead. He felt empty and numb. He wasn't crying, he wasn't angry. He was just . . . nothing. An empty shell of a frog.

"Come on, buddy. We should get going. It's starting to get dark." Croak picked up a lifeless Ribbit and nudged him to his feet.

Croak knew he had to put his grief aside and take it upon himself to lead the two of them to safety for the evening, since Ribbit would be of no help. The problem was, in all of the commotion, he had completely lost his bearings and had no clue which direction to go. He would have liked to head back to the Turtles' house. However, the thick blanket of fog was going to make that nearly impossible. So, Croak decided to cross his fingers, hope for the best, and blindly pick a direction to travel.

After wandering aimlessly through the woods, Croak made the decision to stop navigating and start thinking about building a shelter for the night. A clearing of fog allowed him to see the position of the sun and he knew there were only a few precious hours of daylight left. Maybe three hours, tops. He sat an unresponsive Ribbit on a tree stump and set off to find some fallen branches or large leaves to make a shelter. As he searched the area, Croak noticed a large, thick bush that he thought would be perfect for the night. He ducked into a small hole in the leaves and found the interior to be very spacious and well covered. This was definitely their best bet for the night. He crept out of the bush and gathered up their belongings. Then he swept up his feeble friend, who hadn't moved an inch from the tree stump, and they snuck into the bush to rest.

A tear came to Croak's eyes as he rummaged through Ribbit's pack and found the remains of the food he had packed for the three of them. They were only going to need enough for the two of them now. He gulped down his grief; he had to be strong for Ribbit's sake. Unfortunately, there wasn't much left in the pack, except for a leftover minnow that looked dry, shriveled, and unappealing. Croak was going to have to leave Ribbit in the bush and go in search of food.

"Umm . . . Ribbit?" Croak whispered, as if Ribbit were too fragile to speak to in a normal tone. "I'm gonna go out and get us some food. You just stay here and rest. Maybe try and get some sleep." With that, Croak patted Ribbit softly on the head and squeezed out of the entrance to the bush.

Ribbit sat in a daze, as still as a stone, wearing a haunted expression. His mind was a blur, twisting and writhing its way around what just happened. He closed his eyes and could see Phinn's helpless face staring up at him as he fell. The weight of his grief was crushing his ribcage, making it difficult to breathe. *Phinn's really gone. He's gone and he's never coming back.* With that thought in mind, he finally gave in to his emotions, fell to his knees, and burst violently into tears.

After sobbing his heart out, Ribbit fell into a deep sleep, curled up on the dirt floor. When he opened his eyes, he could see the light of day beginning to fade. How long had he been asleep? He rubbed his swollen, cloudy eyes, and continued to lay curled up on the floor, as if in a trance. The quiet sounds of the forest were suddenly interrupted by voices. He held his breath to listen closely. He could make out Croak's voice, but he wasn't alone. He scooted himself closer to the entrance of the bush, straining his ears. All of a sudden, realization struck him like a bolt of lightning and his heart skipped a beat at the familiar, squeaky voice. *It couldn't be!* Ribbit thought. *It just couldn't be! I must still be dreaming. He's dead. There is no way that it's him.*

There was a rustling at the entrance of the bush as Croak's head popped in. "Ribbit, you aren't going to believe who I ran into!"

As he finished his sentence, another head popped through the entrance of the bush. It was a familiar freckled face that Ribbit could never forget. He rubbed his eyes in disbelief. It was Phinn.

Things Aren't Always What They Seem

"Hey, buddy!" Phinn smiled, squinting at his friend. Having lost his glasses before the big fall, he was nearly as blind as a beetle. "Happy to see me?"

Ribbit stared unblinking. Was he really seeing this or was it his imagination playing tricks on him? Was he still dreaming? Was Phinn a ghost? His mind twisted like a tornado, turning his world upside down.

"What . . . How . . . ?" Ribbit muttered as Croak and Phinn entered the bush, chuckling at Ribbit's surprise.

Phinn strutted over and gave Ribbit a big hug before sitting next to him on the floor. "Well, it's quite an amazing story," he said.

"You see, as I was falling down to my certain death, I shut my eyes and waited for the impact. I felt my body hit something, but it didn't feel anything like I expected it to feel. It was not really painful at all. I actually thought to myself that I was dead and that at least it didn't hurt as bad as I had thought it would. So, I opened my eyes and couldn't see anything except fog and I was totally disappointed. I expected to see heaven. I thought that I would see angel frogs and beautiful clear waters." Phinn mimed angel wings flapping and looked out in the distance as if he were looking out on heaven. Then his eyes returned to Ribbit. "Then I realized that I wasn't dead at all. I was still at the cliff, but I seemed to be flying. I looked down beneath me and realized that I was lying on feathers."

Ribbit gasped, then held his breath as he sat quietly, hanging on to every detail of Phinn's story. Obviously his story was going to have a happy ending because he was here, right in front of Ribbit. Still, he couldn't help but be afraid for Phinn just hearing what had happened.

"Oh, Ribbit, my heart stopped. I knew that I was on top of a big bird, which is never good for a frog." He rolled his eyes. "The whole time I was on his back, I thought how weird it would have been if I survived the fall only to be trapped and eaten by a bird. But what was I going to do? I knew that the bird was flying because I could feel the breeze on my face and I couldn't see below me because of all the fog, so I wasn't about to jump off of it." Phinn stopped and stared at Ribbit. Croak continued to smile intently as if he was in on a great secret.

"And?" Ribbit asked excitedly as he rose shakily to his feet. "What happened? You obviously didn't get eaten, so how'd you escape?"

"Well, that's the best part. The bird, which turned out to be an owl—"

"NO WAY!" Ribbit interrupted. He had read all about owls and heard stories from his father that owls were nasty birds that loved to dine on frogs. So, the thought of Phinn running into an owl sent shivers down his spine.

"Way!" Phinn smiled. "Don't worry, though. He's a nice owl."

"What do you mean he's a nice owl?"

"I mean just that. His name is Oliver, or Ollie for short, and he's a nice owl. He doesn't eat frogs. In fact, he's just outside this bush right now. Why don't you come and meet him, Ribbit?"

Croak was giddy with excitement. He had already met Ollie while he was out searching for food. In fact, it was a good thing that Croak went out for food because Ollie was able to spot him from up above and reunite Phinn with his friends.

"Yep, Ribbit! You gotta meet him. He's really cool," Croak added as he slipped outside.

"Okay," Ribbit said uneasily. He still had a hard time believing that there could be a nice owl.

As he crawled out of the bush, his jaw dropped in amazement at the beauty of the massive bird that stood before him. Ollie's polished cocoa feathers were speckled with white spots, partially hidden by the navy-blue-and-yellow plaid vest he wore. His amber eyes were magnified by tiny metal framed spectacles that sat on the base of his beak. Something about those giant, friendly yellow peepers suggested that he was caring and trustworthy, which was a huge relief to Ribbit.

He stood innocently in front of the three little frogs, trying his best not to look intimidating, for he was no ordinary owl. He was warmhearted, intelligent, caring, and honorable, which were not exactly qualities that one might think of to describe a bird of prey.

"Good evening, Ribbit. Phinnius has told me so much about you," Ollie said smoothly, as he tucked one wing across his body and gave a tiny bow. "It's a pleasure to meet you. My name is Oliver Soarington, but my friends call me Ollie."

"Hello, Ollie," Ribbit responded. He wasn't sure if he should bow back out of respect for the old owl, so he decided to anyway. "Thanks for saving our buddy here," he said, patting Phinn on the back.

Ollie nodded his head as if to say, "you're welcome."

"I just happened to be perched on a tall tree near the cliff," Ollie said, "when I saw the little guy go over. Of course I was going to do what I could to help him out. I know that if I plummeted off a cliff and couldn't fly, I would sure want someone to lend a hand." Ollie gave Phinn a little wink. "Many animals forget that we are all on the same team, just trying to survive in this great big world. We are all brothers and sisters of animal kind and we must never be too busy or self absorbed to help out our family."

Ribbit was already in awe of this wise old owl. He always knew that you were supposed to help others and be a good frog, but he had never heard it put that way before.

"Well, I'm glad that you used your good deed on me," Phinn said sincerely, his eyes glistening.

"Me too, Phinnius," Ollie smiled. "Now, where were you amphibians headed before our little conflict at the cliff back there?"

"Not sure, to be quite honest. We were following some flies." Ribbit shrugged.

"Well, you are definitely going to need a place to stay for the evening," said Ollie. "It's getting dark and I would be happy to put you boys up for the night. I live just north of here." He pointed his beautiful speckled wing toward the distance.

"Wow, that would be great!" Ribbit exclaimed happily. Though he appreciated Croak's efforts to find them shelter for the night, he was not looking forward to sleeping in that bush.

"Awesome. Thanks, Mr. S," Croak said.

"You can call me Ollie, Croak. No need for formalities. Now, finding my home can be a little tricky, so it is important that you listen carefully. I have to fly back now to take care of my children, so you are going to be on your own."

The three frogs nodded.

"Here are the directions: Head north, until you pass two large trees. You'll know them when you see them. Beyond them, there is a path lined with shrubs. They look mysterious and deadly, but that is only to scare away the impure of heart. It's my way of keeping my family protected," he winked. "Once you have followed the path to the end, you will need to find the entrance. Try to see beyond what is right in front of you because appearances can be deceiving. Look for an owl to show you in and we will be waiting. See you there, my little amphibian friends." And with that, Ollie took flight, his enormous wings gliding gracefully as he disappeared into the sky.

"What the heck did that mean?" Croak mumbled, scratching his head in confusion.

"He's making us think, Croak. You didn't think he was just going to give us directions right out? What's the fun in that! It's important that we remember every little detail of what he said," Phinn said.

Ribbit stepped forward. "You have always been good at the details, Phinny boy. So, how about you lead the way, while you," he turned toward Croak. "Keep an eye out for predators. How does that sound, guys?" It felt good to be back to his old self again.

"Yep. Croak on patrol!" Croak shouted, putting his hand up as if he were saluting Ribbit.

"Follow me!" Phinn sung out, marching ahead of the others. He was reveling in being the leader.

Ribbit scampered back into the bush and quickly gathered up the supplies before the frogs headed out on their next mission: finding Ollie's secret home.

*****

Before they knew it, they were at the two large trees Ollie told them about, which acted as a gateway to a path lined with shrubs. Ollie wasn't kidding when he said that the path looked deadly. In fact, downright terrifying would have been a better way to describe it. An eerie, greenish-blue gloom lingered over the forgotten path, creating ghostly shapes and shadows. Twisted shrubs, like hundreds of sharp nails, pressed in from the sides, threatening that once the frogs stepped foot on this path, there was no turning back.

The three frogs gazed at the gloomy path, as if they didn't know what to do next. "Well, looks like that's the end of that. There's no way we're going on that road of death," Phinn announced.

"Yeah, this looks pretty bad," Ribbit said. He squinted, hoping that his eyes were playing tricks on him and that the path really wasn't all that scary, but he couldn't make out anything in the fog. From where he stood, the path looked as if it were lined with long, skeletal fingers just waiting to snatch them up. He shook his head. "But why would Ollie save your life, just to turn around and try and kill us? Think about it; if he really wanted us dead, he could have eaten us by the bush back there. I mean, no one was there to stop him."

"He's got a point," Croak said, his big eyes looking directly at Phinn.

"Ugh . . . I guess you're right," Phinn gulped. "Ollie's a friend. I'll probably regret saying this if we get eaten by something out there, but let's do this."

The three little frogs walked warily down the daunting path. They hugged tightly to each other, staying as far away from the spiky branches as possible. Ribbit could feel Phinn trembling beside him, barely keeping in stride. He turned his head and looked proudly at Croak, who was so alert and ready to defend that he flinched at every bird chirp and creak of the trees moving in the wind.

The path stretched as far as they could see, as if it were never ending. The sun hung low in the sky; night would be falling soon. The tree branches high above sketched the ground before them with flickering shadows like demons dancing merrily and welcoming them to their doom. Ribbit was sure there were predators looming behind every turn or lurking just ahead, masked by the thick fog, awaiting their arrival. All he could do was cling tightly to his friends, hold his breath, and wish for the best.

After a while, the fog began to clear and Ribbit could see something up ahead. He cried out in glee and started to run. He could not get off that path quick enough. Phinn and Croak followed closely behind, letting out cheers that they had survived the journey. They came to an abrupt stop at a large brick wall covered in ivy. It consumed the area with its massive size, as if standing guard of what lay behind.

"Well, what now?" Croak asked, shrugging his shoulders.

"I . . . I . , . I don't know," Phinn stammered. For once, his knowledge of the details was failing him.

"Okay, let's just take a moment, guys," Ribbit said. He turned to Phinn. "Now what exactly did Ollie say to do next?"

"Well, he said that things aren't always as they seem and we're supposed to find the door to his home somewhere around here.

And something about an owl showing us in?" Phinn looked around. "I'm not seeing any owls around here. Maybe he forgot to come and let us in?"

"I suppose. Looks like we are going to have to find the door ourselves," Ribbit sighed.

The three frogs searched and searched a seemingly endless wall of ivy, looking for whatever clues that they could find. Phinn leaned his face as close as he could to the wall and squinted; but without his glasses, he probably wasn't going to be much help. Croak wasn't having any luck either.

"Ugh . , . all I see are plants, plants, plants!" a frustrated Croak shouted, kicking the dirt beneath his feet.

"Calm down, Croak. Remember, Ollie said this would be tricky. Of course there isn't going to be an obvious door. He said that he had to keep this place private and away from evildoers. So, we need to look more carefully." Phinn said.

They went back to searching. Just when Ribbit was about to give up, he noticed one of the bricks on the wall had a carving on it. He leaned in closer and was able to make out the clear detailed carving of an owl. *A clue!*

"Hey, guys! I think I found something!" Ribbit called out, waving his friends to the center of the wall.

"What? What did you find?" Phinn gasped for air from leaping over to Ribbit so quickly.

"Yeah, what is it?" Croak wheezed, his voice alive with excitement once more.

"I found a brick with a carving of an owl. I think it's a clue."

"That's what Ollie meant by an owl showing us in. It wasn't a real owl, but a carving of an owl." Phinn's eyes gleamed.

"So what do we do now?" Croak asked.

"Maybe if I just . . ." Ribbit slipped his scrawny fingers around the edges of the brick and began to jiggle. The brick loosened and slid out from the wall, revealing an old brass key underneath. He held up the old key, staring at it in amazement. He felt as if he had just found buried treasure, which, in a way, he had.

"Whoa!" Croak gasped, leaning in to get a closer look at the old key.

"You did it, Rib! You found a key! That means there's gotta be a door or a gate around here somewhere!" Phinn exclaimed excitedly.

All three frogs gripped the wall, feeling every inch in search of a door, but the ivy's leafy cloak made its discovery nearly impossible. After a while, Croak gave up, sat on the ground, took out some stones from his vest pocket, and threw them aimlessly at the wall. Each stone hit with a loud *clank* of stone on brick, until one stone hit with a *thud*. Ribbit and Phinn stopped working and stared at each other with wide eyes. Croak grabbed another stone out of his vest pocket and aimed for the exact same spot on the wall. He threw the stone and heard the same *thud* that was unmistakably the sound of stone hitting wood.

All three frogs bounded over to the wall, pushed aside the overgrown ivy, and delighted in the sight of an old wooden door hiding amid the foliage.

"Good work, Croak!" Ribbit leapt in the air with excitement.

"Try the key! Try the key!" Phinn cried, pointing anxiously at the lock.

Ribbit took the old brass key out of his shorts pocket. His hand was trembling with excitement as he placed the key in the keyhole of the wooden door. It fit. Ribbit slowly turned the key and with a loud creaking noise, the door opened.

The Enchanted Meadow

They had opened the door to a gorgeous meadow teeming with color and echoing with the gleeful sound of nature's critters at play. Dazzling orange, red, purple, and yellow wildflowers blossomed everywhere. They gently swayed in the soft breeze, their sweet aroma drifting in the air.

A jumble of young animals including a skunk, a squirrel, a rabbit, and a hedgehog scampered about on the lush green grass. They were cheerfully playing games of tag and acorn catch. Beyond them a small otter and a miniature yellow duck splashed happily in the cool waters of a babbling brook that wound its way through the meadow. Above the excitement, colorful butterflies fluttered in the purple and pink streaked sky above, while bluebirds flitted about, releasing a chorus of twitters and peeps in the golden sunlit meadow.

Directly in front of them, purple blossoms meandered up a gazebo that housed four twig chairs with plump pillows. A young raccoon and a small opossum snoozed in two of the twig chairs. On a small tree stump in the middle of the gazebo sat a large pitcher of iced tea and a plate of tree-shaped cookies.

A tiny voice snapped the frogs out of their amazement. "They're here! They're here!" the little skunk sang out. All at once, the creatures stopped what they were doing and scurried over to meet their new visitors.

"Papa! Papa! Come quick! They're here!" squeaked the tiny squirrel as he roused his slumbering friends, the raccoon and the opossum, to come and join in all the excitement.

The little critters sprinted over to the three frogs and encircled them in a frenzy of cheerful greetings. It almost made Ribbit dizzy watching them dance and parade about.

"Hi! Hi! Hi! Check this out!" the raccoon shouted, as he cartwheeled clumsily in circles. He quickly became a black and tan blur.

"Hi-o!" the squirrel cried out, bouncing sprightly around the three frogs.

"Who are they?" the opossum asked, her face puckering with a look of utter confusion.

"Remember, they're the frogs that Papa met over by the cliffs?" The skunk pointed at them with her tiny pink finger.

"You know, the brainless ones that almost fell off the edge?" the hedgehog sneered, chuckling. Ribbit could tell that he wasn't going to care for this hedgehog much.

"Hello there, my amphibian friends!" a smooth, gentle voice sang out, as the gorgeous spotted owl swooped down from the treetop of a strong, majestic oak tree high in the lilac sky. It dominated the area with its gnarled branches twisting and turning in all directions. Each of its four stories boasted arched windows decorated with lace curtains, billowing in the breeze. In the front of the great tree, tiny wooden stairs led up to an ancient oval door, adorned with fancy woodcarvings, and a small peephole in the middle. Candlelight flickered within the front windows. At the highest point there was a lookout tower, which is where Ribbit suspected Ollie had been quietly observing them since their arrival.

"Welcome to our Enchanted Meadow," Ollie said warmly as he landed gracefully on the ground.

Enchanted Meadow. That pretty much sums it up, Ribbit thought to himself.

"This place in incredible!" Ribbit exclaimed, taking another moment to absorb the beauty of his surroundings.

"That's an understatement," Phinn added.

"Why, thank you friends. We think it's pretty magnificent. But the best part of the Enchanted Meadow is right here," Ollie said, staring lovingly down at the little animals around him.

"Ribbit, Croak, Phinnius, these are my children," Ollie announced, using his giant wings to gather up the little critters. "This little one here is Squirt," he pointed at the small skunk, who gave a little bow. "This fella is Bristle," he said pointing to the hedgehog

Ribbit wasn't so keen on. The little hedgehog nodded his head in hello. "Over here we have Dizzy. She can do an impressive whirl hanging from her tail." The opossum, still looking a bit confused, just stared at the frogs with no gesture of hello. Ollie leaned in. "She's a bit on the quiet side, but we find it rather endearing," he whispered quietly to the frogs, covering his mouth so that the others couldn't hear.

"What about me! What about me!" The little squirrel squealed, jumping up and down and waving his arms frantically.

"Oh, I could never forget you, Scooter," Ollie explained, giving a little chuckle. "He is quite the little ball of energy." Scooter began springing and leaping through the air, waving his arms in hello. Ollie gave him a moment before he introduced the next animals. "Over here, we have Twitch." The little rabbit trembled and in the blink of an eye darted behind Ollie. "Aw, he's just a little shy. No need to be offended. He's like this with all new animals," he continued. "This big fella here is Chubby. He is the eldest of our children." Ollie gave the otter a gentle pat on the head with his soft feathers. Chubby stepped forward and gave each of the three frogs a stern handshake. He was clearly the responsible one of the group.

"Chubby has taken our youngest child, Peanut, under his wing . . . or should I say, under his arm," Ollie gave a playful smile. "Come on out little Peanut and say hello to our guests." The tiny lemon-colored duck peeked out from behind Chubby's leg. She had been hiding there since the moment the frogs had arrived.

"Hello!" Peanut giggled, her soft wispy feathers gently waving.

"Next, we have Bandit." Ollie walked over and put his spotted wings on the shoulders of the little raccoon. "Bandit is an astounding dancer. He really has a talent." He gave the frogs a little wink. "Why don't you show them some of your routine?" Ollie whispered to Bandit, who quickly scuttled out in front of the children and began to show off his best moves. Ribbit, Phinn, and Croak had to hide their chuckles. Bandit could not have been more uncoordinated. Ribbit understood why Ollie had winked. It was obvious by Bandit's display that he had no idea just how terrible of a dancer he was thanks to the support he received from his family. They all encouraged him and cheered him on despite his horrendous dance moves.

"Last, but not least we have my wife, Ophelia. We call her 'Momma' around here. She's the glue that keeps this family together. She's inside preparing some supper for us all. You'll meet her momentarily," Ollie said proudly, gazing at the giant oak, which was being lit up room by room with a gentle glow of candlelight.

"Wow! You have a very unique family, Ollie. It's great to meet you all," Ribbit said, looking each one of the children in the eyes. Ribbit had never seen a more diverse group of animals living together and calling themselves a family. It almost surprised him how warm and tingly it made him feel to see all of these different animals living together as brothers and sisters. They didn't see themselves as being different from each other. They saw themselves as a family.

Watching the little children, so bubbly and full of life, reminded Ribbit of Zippy. He wondered how she was doing without him. Did she think he had abandoned her and the family? The thought made his heart heavy. He hated leaving her in such a rush, but he knew she would understand one day.

"Thank you, Ribbit. We take a lot of pride in our family. Well . . ." Ollie's eyes glimpsed toward the sky. "The sun has almost set and I do believe it is time for supper. Why don't we all go in and see what Momma has prepared for us to eat?" Ollie announced, nudging his children with his wings. The children skittered along the stone path, up the old wooden stairs, and into the giant oak that was now completely lit up with a warm amber glow from within, while Ribbit, Phinn, Croak, and Ollie took a more leisurely stroll inside. Since the moment he had laid eyes on all of the children, Ribbit was curious as to why they were all there. How did Ollie collect all of these different animals to make up his family? And more importantly, why? He knew that he had to ask or his curiosity was going to get the best of him.

"Umm . . . Ollie? I hope you don't mind me asking you something," Ribbit said quietly as they headed down the stone path.

"Ask away, my little friend. I find it wonderful that you are inquisitive. That is a sign of a true thinker, Ribbit. So, what is it that you wish to know?" Ollie responded in a smooth tone that made Ribbit feel comfortable.

"Well, I was just wondering. Why do you have so many different kinds of children living here?"

"Ah, I had a feeling you would be wondering about that," he smiled. "Well, the truth is that the Enchanted Meadow is a sort of orphanage, I suppose. We really don't like to think of it that way because the word *orphan* is often associated with children who have no parents. These children have parents because they have us. But, I guess if you were looking for a formal definition, they are orphans in that their biological parents are no longer around. Does that answer your question, Ribbit?"

Before Ribbit could respond, Phinn chimed in, "But that doesn't explain how they came to be here."

"Very astute, Phinnius. I suppose my response to that varies for each child. For instance, Momma and I came across Squirt when we were out on a twilight flight for exercise. Momma was the one who spotted her crying in a field, completely alone and unsupervised. When we swooped down, we discovered that the poor thing was terrified because her mother had gone out to look for food and never returned. Poor little Squirt was left on her own for two whole days before we came along. So, naturally, we took Squirt back to our home and searched tirelessly for her mother for days. Unfortunately, we never did find out what happened to Squirt's mother. We fear for the worst, but still keep a wary eye out today. So that, my friends, is how our little Squirt came to us some six months ago. The others each have their own tales, but the one thing that they all have in common is that they needed someone to look out for them and give them the love that only a parent can give, which is exactly what we are doing."

Ribbit's heart melted.

"You're a good owl," Phinn said, wiping tears from his eyes.

"No, I'm just doing what any animal should do; looking out for my fellow animals," Ollie said humbly, as he opened the arched door and escorted his new friends into the warmth of his home.

Dinner with the Soarington's

Momma gave Ribbit, Phinn, and Croak a very warm welcome and ushered them to a special spot at the table. She was just as kind and wonderful as Ribbit had thought she'd be. From the way she gently greeted her children to the way she lovingly placed the food on the table, it was apparent that she delighted in cooking and caring for her family.

The dining room was very large and illuminated by the warm glow from candles that flickered on a low-hanging chandelier, as well as from a stone fireplace that housed a crackling fire. Momma had insisted the frogs sit next to Ollie at the head of the enormous dining room table, which looked as if it were a large log that had been cut in half to make a flat tabletop. It took up most of the room, stretching from wall to wall, and it comfortably sat the whole Soarington family, plus a few amphibian friends. They took their seat on a long wooden bench that stretched along the dinner table. There was a matching bench on the other side and two wooden chairs at the heads of the table. On the gigantic table sat a large array of foods, such as fish, smoked grasshoppers, spiced moths, sliced apples, a hay salad, bread, and steamed acorns. There was something on the table for everyone to enjoy.

Ollie and Momma made their way around the table, making sure each of their children had washed their hands and had everything they needed for their meal. As Momma passed by, the sweet smell of lavender followed her. When the children on her side of the table had all been checked, she took out a large wooden spoon from one of the many pockets on her pink lacy apron and stirred the sliced apples, which were lightly dusted with cinnamon. When she was pleased with the blend, she left the spoon inside the bowl and wiped her hands on her apron. Ribbit's eye was drawn to the variety of things she had stuffed in its small pockets: napkins, extra utensils, bandages, and even what appeared to be some small candies for her little ones. She was ready for anything.

Ollie and Momma finally took their seats at the heads of table. Ollie unfolded the napkin from his plate and gently laid it across his lap. Momma and the children did the same, so the frogs decided to as well. Before the meal began, Momma said a quick word of gratitude for the food before them and how pleased they were to welcome their new friends into their home. Ribbit blushed, Croak nodded, and Phinn smiled in return. Then Ollie announced that everyone could begin eating. Food was passed around the table as the animals all eagerly loaded up their plates. Phinn decided to play it safe and spooned only two different foods on his plate: fish and bread. Ribbit, however, wanted to try a little bit of everything. He figured, he probably would never have the opportunity to eat these foods again, so he'd better try them all while he had the chance. Croak did the same, though his plate was much more full than Ribbit's.

A frenzied chatter and clanking of dishes and utensils filled the air with its melody like an evening song. Ribbit enjoyed sitting quietly and observing the unusual owl family as they talked about their day and discussed their interests. What he thought most fascinating was how Ollie and Momma were so attentive to each of their eight children. All of them could be speaking at once, which often was the case, yet Ollie and Momma would respond to every statement, letting their children know that what they say and think is important. It was clear that although this was a big family, none of the children felt that they weren't heard or that they didn't get the attention that they needed. This truly was one big, happy family.

"Ribbit, Phinn, Croak, are you all enjoying your meal?" Ollie asked, being sure to include his new visitors in all of the commotion.

"It's fantastic!" Ribbit said, his mouth full of Momma's spiced moths. His meal was so good, it was a close second to his mother's fly stew.

"This is excellent, Momma. You truly are a magician in the kitchen," Phinn exclaimed, rubbing his full stomach in satisfaction.

"Yep. This grub is awesome," Croak added, his mouth still full of food. Talking with his mouth full was a bad habit that Croak's parents had been hassling him about for years.

"So sweet of you to say," Momma blushed. She was as humble as she was caring.

"Yes, Momma, you are something else," Ollie said, staring lovingly at his blushing wife. "Children, why don't you run along, put on your pajamas, brush your teeth, and meet me in the library."

The children all jumped out of their seats and bounded up the staircase, their loud, squeaky voices becoming more distant, until all was quiet in the great dining room.

"So, my little amphibian friends, we never discussed the reason why you were wandering around the woods alone earlier today. Where are you from and what is it that you seek?" Ollie asked curiously, his round face cocked slightly to the side.

"We all live together in a small town called Lily Pad Hollow. We left there three days ago because we're on a mission," Ribbit announced. He was feeling a bit hesitant to tell Ollie of their plans to find out what happened to all of the flies. Although he had always felt confident about their great voyage, Ollie was incredibly wise and Ribbit was afraid of what he might say. What if he told them that it was a silly mission for some little frogs to go on? What if he told them that they simply wouldn't be able to pull it off? That would break Ribbit's heart. Suddenly, he felt more like a child playing sword fights and less like a hero trying to save the day. His hands began to sweat and his heart began to race because he knew that

Ollie was going to ask about their mission and pass some sort of judgment.

"Hmm . . . interesting. So, what type of a mission are you on?" Ollie inquired, his round face still cocked to the side.

"Well . . . well . . ." Ribbit stammered, his heart in his throat.

"We're looking for flies," Croak blurted, unintentionally showing off his mouth full of smoked grasshoppers.

Ribbit's pulse quickened. Why did Croak have to blurt it out like that?

"Flies? So you all are on a mission to find flies?" Ollie asked, his face illuminated by the sputtering fire. His face was expressionless, and Ribbit couldn't tell what he was thinking. He decided that he had better explain so that they didn't sound like some reckless, immature frogs who were out simply looking for some flies to eat.

"And mosquitoes, too!" Phinn said, hoping that adding mosquitoes would make it sound like a more concrete plan.

"What they mean to say," Ribbit spoke out, his hands trembling, "is that Lily Pad Hollow is in trouble. You see, we eat mostly flies there and for some reason the flies have stopped coming recently. My mother's job is in danger and the whole town is starting to shut down without them. We knew that if something wasn't done, frogs could starve and the home that we love so much could . . . could . . ." Ribbit hesitated. He was racking his brain for the right words to say and in his nervousness was drawing a blank. After a moment's pause, he added, "Well, I guess you could say that the town would die."

Ollie remained quiet—painstakingly quiet—rubbing his chin with a feather from his magnificent wing. Finally, after a moment of silence, he spoke out. "Wow. That is quite the predicament you have there, friends," he said calmly. "What is it that you plan to do to save that wonderful town of yours?"

Ribbit also took a moment to pause before responding. He wanted to take his time, like Ollie had, to make sure that he was going to say the right words. He didn't want to rush his response and come off looking stupid. Phinn and Croak were both staring at Ribbit with a blank look on their faces. He knew that they were looking at him because this had been his mission. He had been the one who insisted on leaving Lily Pad Hollow and he was the one who was supposed to have a plan. The problem was he didn't.

"Well, our plan is to go out exploring and looking for flies, and then follow them to find out where they are going." The words came spilling out of Ribbit's mouth as if he could no longer contain them. His body tensed up awaiting the flurry of questions that he anticipated Ollie would throw at him. Questions like, "What happens if you don't find any flies?" "What are you going to do when you figure out where the flies are going?" "Why would you go on a mission like this without an adult?" and "What makes you think that you three young frogs can do this on your own?" These were all questions that Ribbit was afraid of because he had no answers to them. No answers, at least, that he felt would be good enough for

Ollie's brilliant reasoning. He could hardly say, "I'm going on this expedition because I always pretended to be some great hero and I wanted to act it out in real life." No, that would just sound silly.

Once again, Ollie sat his in chair, stroking his chin with his soft, spotted wing. His moments of silence made Ribbit nervous, so he felt relieved when the wise owl finally spoke. "I have to say, I really admire you three frogs for taking some risks to save your town. It is very brave of you to head out into the world, not knowing what to expect or what trials will come your way. Although you may not have a tangible plan, your enthusiasm and dedication to your mission will lead you where you need to go."

A grin overtook Ribbit's face and a jolt of excitement rushed through his body. The wisest person he had ever met not only understood where he was coming from, but also supported his efforts. He couldn't ask for a more motivating response.

Ollie looked at Momma, who gave him a nod of support. "Now, what is it that we can do to help?" he asked.

"Really, you want to help?" Phinn asked, his hand hitting his fork and launching it across the table toward an unflinching Croak.

"Of course we'd like to help out our new friends. Your town is in trouble and the more of us who are working to find a solution, the better," Ollie grinned, pushing his spectacles a little higher on his beak.

"Wow, that would be great! Thank you!" Ribbit said. "I'm just not sure what we need help with right now. As you can tell, we don't have much of a plan."

Ollie smiled and said, "Some of the greatest things in life have happened without a plan. It was never our plan to have eight children and live in this meadow, but it's the most wonderful unplanned thing that has ever happened to us," Ollie placed his wing on top of Ophelia's and they exchanged glances. "You never know what life will throw your way. Take our meeting, for example. You couldn't have possibly predicted you would be here, and now there is something I can offer you that you cannot offer yourselves." He raised his eyebrows above his big yellow eyes.

"Like what?" Croak asked, his mouth and plate finally empty.

"Like these." Ollie spread out his wings. "I can fly you high above the treetops. Hopefully there we will have a better view of those flies you so desperately seek."

"Whoa!" Croak grunted.

"I think you will really enjoy the ride. Ollie's quite skilled at soaring. It runs in the family, which is why our last name is Soarington." Momma chuckled. "You should have seen him in his heyday. He could fly circles around any bird I knew. He's still got a few tricks up his sleeve, even in his golden years." Momma gave her husband a little kiss and smoothed out her apron before walking into the kitchen to prepare some cocoa.

"Wow! This is more than we could have asked for! We really appreciate it, Ollie," Ribbit added, trying to contain the high-pitched squeal building up inside of him. He was going to fly on a real-life owl!

"It's the least I can do," Ollie said warmly, taking off his spectacles and rubbing them on his plaid vest.

Ribbit had no idea, in that very moment, how much Ollie's offer was going to change his life.

Ollie's Story

Despite their offering to help, Momma and Ollie insisted that the boys relax by the fire while they prepared the cocoa. Being the good frogs they were, they did what they were told. The three of them sat on the hearth with their back to the fire, staring out of the large picture window of the dining room. They were almost as entranced by the beauty of the meadow at nighttime as they had been during the day. The harvest moon cast a magical glow over the quiet meadow, creating unique patterns and shadows on the ground. Fireflies twinkled and darted about, putting on a show against the black backdrop of night. All that could be heard was the crackling of the fire, the symphony of chirping from the crickets outside, and the gentle cooing of Momma in the kitchen.

When the cocoa was ready, the boys helped Ollie and Momma carry the thirteen mugs of hot cocoa all the way up to the very top of the old oak tree. They climbed a spiral staircase up three flights before reaching the library. The first floor consisted of a large bedroom lined with bunk beds where all of the children slept. It was a fun room, filled with toys; the walls plastered with drawings and artwork the children had created. The second floor of the owl house was Ollie and Momma's master suite. They also had a stone fireplace and a large round bed that looked cushy and plush. Ribbit got an itch to go and jump on their bed, letting his body sink into its fluffiness, but he knew that would be totally inappropriate. He still couldn't help but imagine how fun a pillow fight on that bed would be.

On the third floor of the great oak was an old library. This library had a feeling of timeless tradition. The room was enveloped in rich dark wood, polished to a glossy shine. The walls were lined with shelves housing row upon row of books of every size and every color—beckoning for someone to pick them up and delve into the endless knowledge they held. The books' worn appearance gave them a sense of importance, like they were overflowing with secrets and truth that should be read over and over again. In the corner was a window seat with a quilted throw and fluffy pillows that invited settling in with a warm cup of tea. Next to the window seat was a rustic, rounded door leading to a wooden balcony where Ollie could look out over the meadow, keeping an eye out for trouble. On the opposite end of the room, a large, polished grandfather clock towered in the corner, its deep chimes resonating on the hour. Next to the grandfather clock stood a massive stone fireplace surrounded by four cozy, overstuffed chairs that were arranged in a crescent to face the crackling fire.

The room smelled of leather and old books. It was the smell of literature, the smell of learning, the smell of knowledge. Ribbit closed his eyes and took in a deep breath.

His moment of relaxation was halted as the little children pranced into the library, looking snug in their cozy pajamas. They each took a cup of hot cocoa from the large silver platter, a look of delight on their tiny faces, and they grabbed a spot on the overstuffed couches and chairs. Ribbit guessed this was a nightly ritual, as they each took their own spot without so much as a peep or an argument about who got to sit where. The frogs decided to lounge on the plush carpet of the library floor, so as not to put anyone out of their usual seat.

"Alright, my little children. Whose turn is it to pick a book this evening?" Ollie asked, sitting in a large, worn, brown leather chair that was at the head of the room. Momma sat in a similar chair to his left.

"Oh, oh! It's my turn!" Scooter cried out, as he scampered over to the wall of books and stood pondering which story to choose. After a few moments of scanning the shelves, he picked an old, red, leather bound book and happily handed it to Momma.

"Good choice, my love," she said, giving Scooter a gentle kiss on the cheek before he shuffled back to his seat. "Scooter has chosen *Porcupine Finds His Way*."

"Oooh! I love this story!" Squirt exclaimed, her pink hands snug around her steaming cup of cocoa.

"Me, too!" Chubby added, his mouth lined with a frothy cocoa mustache.

Everyone sat quietly, mesmerized by Momma's reading. She was an excellent storyteller. She gave all of the characters their own voices and she knew just when to pause to create anticipation. She even used her acting skills to act out the scenes of the story. It was fascinating! One minute she was a nice, gentle porcupine and the next she was an evil shrew plotting to take over the world. She was truly a one-owl show.

Ribbit found himself so entranced by the story that he completely forgot to drink his hot cocoa. He even found he was holding his breath when the story got good. He could see why the owl family had so many books in their library. Ribbit could have stayed in that room and listened to Momma read all night long.

When the story was over, all of the little critters clapped in approval. They patted Scooter on the back and told him what a great story he had chosen.

Before putting the book away, Momma asked her children if they could tell her the moral of the story. They all raised their hands, eager to participate. She called on Twitch to come up and he anxiously hopped to the front of the room with Ollie and Momma. He stood there, silent for a moment, while the other children shouted words of encouragement. Quietly, Twitch whispered that the moral of the story was to always tell the truth. The children cheered while

Momma and Ollie hugged their little rabbit son. Mama nuzzled her face against the top of his soft head, right between his floppy ears, and whispered how proud she was of him.

"Alright, my darlings. Time for bed," Momma cooed, as she rounded up the little ones. Each small animal ran up to Ollie and gave him a gentle kiss good night on his soft, feathery cheek. Then they waved good night to Ribbit, Croak, and Phinn and scampered off to bed. Ribbit could hear their voices get fainter as they bounded down the stairs and into their quiet, cozy bedroom.

The library that was just teeming with energy moments ago now felt empty and still. Ribbit, Croak, Phinn, and Ollie sat quietly, listening to the tick-tock of the old grandfather clock, the crackling of the warm fire, and the distant sound of the cricket's song in the meadow.

"Hey, Ollie. I have a question for you," Ribbit said, breaking the silence.

"Ask away, my friend," Ollie responded, his voice like velvet.

"Please tell me if I'm wrong here, but I thought that owls were awake during the night and asleep during the day. What is it they call that again?"

"Nocturnal," Phinn whispered in Ribbit's direction.

"Yeah, that's it. Nocturnal. I thought owls were nocturnal." Ribbit didn't know why he asked that question. What did it matter if Ollie was awake during the day and asleep during the night? Did that make any difference to the type of owl he was? No. So why did he care about Ollie's sleeping patterns? I guess his curiosity just got the best of him.

"Yes, you are correct. Owls are nocturnal," Ollie answered, nodding his head. He clearly wasn't bothered by the question at all, which was a relief to Ribbit. He didn't want Ollie to think that he was prying.

"You're an owl. How come you aren't nocturminal or whatever it's called?" Croak interrogated, looking suspiciously at Ollie as if he were breaking some great animal rule or something.

"Well, that's a very reasonable question, Croak. I do believe that was the original question that Ribbit had intended on asking. Am I right in that assumption, Ribbit?" Ollie asked.

"Umm . . . yeah. I guess I was wondering why you came and rescued us when it was still daytime and why you are all turning in for bed now that it is nighttime if you are supposed to be nocturnal?" Ribbit explained.

Ollie paused for a moment, as usual, and thought carefully before speaking. "I presume you have noticed that I am no ordinary owl," he stated confidently.

"You could say that again," Phinn murmured, drinking the last of his cocoa, which was lukewarm now. Croak nodded his head in agreement.

Ollie rustled his feathers in his worn leather chair and sat up straight to address the boys. "Well, then. Let me explain to you why I am the way I am."

Ribbit could tell this was going to be a good story, so he set down his mug, crossed his legs, and sat up as straight as he possibly could, ready to listen. Phinn and Croak did the same, their eyes sparkling with eagerness.

"You see, a long time ago, I was just like any other spotted owl. I slumbered during the day and soared the skies in the darkness of night, hunting for prey. Regrettably, I feasted like an ordinary spotted owl as well. I used to hunt and eat everything from frogs like yourselves . . ."

A shiver ran down Ribbit's spine. Phinn grasped his arm tightly and he heard Croak gulp loudly at the sound of those words. *He actually ate frogs like us?*

". . . to rodents and small animals." Ollie peered down at his stomach. A look of shame crossed his face as he removed the small spectacles from his beak and began to wipe them clean with a small cloth. "Now, this is not something I am proud of. In fact, you could say it is the one thing that I am most ashamed of in my life. It distresses me to even think about the poor animals whose lives were torn apart by my actions." He sat silently for a moment, his eyes drifting out the large arched window, into the darkness beyond. Then he gave a deep sigh and stared back at the boys with his friendly yellow eyes. The same eyes that assured Ribbit from the very beginning that Ollie could be trusted.

"However," he said, straightening his plaid vest, "I try not to dwell on the past. What's done is done and there is nothing I can do to change what happened. All I can try to do now is forgive myself

150

for the wrongs that I have committed and use them as a lesson to guide me. I'm not saying that it excuses my actions, but it is the only way I know how to cope with it and come out of everything as a better owl."

"So, what happened? You just woke up one morning and decided you didn't want to live that way anymore?" Ribbit questioned, his gaze fixed on Ollie.

"Oh no, my friend. That is a great story indeed. A story I think that you will take particular delight in." Ollie grinned and placed his now spotless spectacles back on the crown of his beak.

"Tell it! Tell it!" Croak chanted, his body jolting up and down wildly. Phinn joined in the chanting.

"Come on! We wanna hear it!" Ribbit cried out, his knees bouncing up and down in their crossed position.

"Ask and you shall receive. Now, where to begin," he pondered, rubbing his giant, silky wing along the crease of his chin. "Ah, yes. It all started . . ."

As Ollie spoke, his words transported the frogs to a time long, long ago. It was twilight and the sky was streaked with orange and pink, as a much younger Ollie was just waking and preparing to search for his breakfast. He explained how he had perched himself high among the trees where he spotted a group of happy frogs, singing merrily, dancing in the warm summer breeze, and relaxing by a crackling bonfire. From his point of view, it was a delightful froggy buffet! So he took off from his perch and headed toward his next meal. As he swooped in on his prey, his left wing was suddenly struck by something that caused him to tumble out of the sky. He plummeted down, down, down, his eyesight a blur of pink, orange, green, and brown. He knew what the pink, orange, and green were (the sky and the frogs), but he couldn't tell what or who the brown was.

He hit the ground hard with a loud thud. Mustering up all of the energy he had left, he turned himself over to face his attacker. He never expected it to be a hawk. And this was not a normal hawk. This hawk was gigantic! A real monster! His wingspan must have been four feet wide. His black beady eyes stared lifelessly at an injured, young Ollie, sizing up his competition. Ollie's only explanation for the attack was that the hawk must have spotted the frogs as well and wanted to rid himself of any competitors. Whatever the reason, he had Ollie right where he wanted him.

Ollie struggled to pull himself up, hoping to make a quick get-away since there was no possible way that he could take on a hawk of that size. However, the hawk had other plans in mind. As Ollie attempted to take off into the sky, the giant hawk snapped his razor-sharp beak around Ollie's foot, slicing off one of his small brown toes. Once again, Ollie hurdled toward the ground, hitting the dirt hard, pain overwhelming his senses. Injured and bleeding, he knew that he was now at the mercy of the hawk. He could hear the beating of the colossal hawk's wings close to his head and was positive that another attack was coming. Ollie closed his eyes, curled his body into a ball and braced himself for the final blow that would probably end his life.

As he lay there trembling in fear, he suddenly heard a rustling sound from the bushes behind him, followed by the whizzing sound of something flying quickly over his head. The mammoth hawk let out a thunderous squawk as if he had been hit. Ollie opened his eyes and turned to see what had happened. Before him, the giant hawk hopped angrily on one foot. Just then, Ollie heard the whizzing sound overhead again. But this time it wasn't just one object, it was many. From behind the bushes, many small jagged stones shot through the air at the big hawk. Luckily, being ambushed by tiny stones diverted the hawk's attention away from Ollie and Ollie was able to stand up and ready himself in case of another attack. Although the hawk tried desperately to shield himself, one of the sharp stones launched through the air, hitting him square in the eye. The hawk screeched out, writhing in pain. Ollie could see that the rock had taken his eye out. Quick as a blink, the hawk took off into the sky, leaving Ollie behind. Ollie gave out a joyful cheer and yelled at the hawk that he better not come around these parts again. He was feeling on top of the world! He had survived and it was all thanks to whoever threw the stones. Ollie rushed toward the bush, expecting to find a fellow owl or maybe a friendly deer. He never would have guessed who his saviors would be.

"Well, who was it? Was it Momma?" Ribbit asked excitedly.

"No. It was, in fact, the very frogs whom I had been scheming against." Ollie smiled.

"No way!" Croak whispered, his round eyes even larger than usual.

"Yes, indeed. Those frogs saved my life. They saw what had happened and even though I was their enemy, they still came to my aid. When I asked them why, they simply responded that helping out an animal in need was what every animal should do."

"That's incredible! Saved by frogs! Who would have thunk it!" Phinn exclaimed, his mouth open in astonishment.

"And ever since that day, I vowed to never eat another animal again and to treat all animals, regardless of their phylum and species, with kindness and respect. Thus, the reason for my home here." Ollie continued, spreading his wing in a circle and pointing to his surroundings. "I have made it my life's purpose to help all creatures in need. It just so happened that I met a wonderful life companion in Ophelia to help me on my journey. She and I have changed our ways, including our diets and being nocturnal, for the sake of our children."

"Wow! That's an amazing story, Ollie." Ribbit smiled, his eyes glistening in adoration for the old owl. "It sounds almost too good to be true."

"Wait a minute. That's just it. How do we know that it is all the truth?" Phinn asked, looking suspiciously at Ollie with one brow raised. "I mean, don't get me wrong. It's a fascinating story. Just, how do we know that it all really happened?"

All three frogs stared intently at Ollie, waiting for an answer, waiting for a response.

"I'm glad that you analyze what you are told, Phinnius. It is a true mark of intellect. As for my proof, how will this do?" Ollie said calmly, lifting up his feathers to reveal his feet. Sure enough, one of the toes on his left foot was missing.

"Good enough for me!" Croak spat out, as they all enjoyed a chuckle.

Just then the old grandfather clock gave a deep, resonating chime, signaling that it was ten o'clock.

"My goodness, look at the time. I guess the proverb rings true: Time sure does fly in the presence of great friends. Let us turn in now." Ollie announced, as he gathered up some warm, quilted blankets and soft, fluffy pillows so the boys could make up their beds.

"I hope you don't mind sleeping up here in the library. Unfortunately, we have quite the full house." Ollie muttered.

"Not at all, Ollie. We're going to be very comfortable up here," Ribbit insisted, as he made up his bed on the plush carpet in front of the crackling fire. "Thanks again for having us. We really appreciate it." The other boys echoed his sentiment.

"The pleasure is mine," Ollie cooed. "Now get some rest. Tomorrow brings anew." And with that, Ollie crept out of the room, leaving the three frogs nestled together under a warm quilt on the floor of the great library. Ribbit lay awake for a moment, listening to the symphony of crickets in the Enchanted Meadow and the crackling of the glowing embers in the fireplace. He closed his eyes and snuggled in-between his two best buddies. He would need his rest. Tomorrow was going to be a big day.

The Great Flight

After eating a hearty dragonfly pancake breakfast, Ollie told Ribbit, Phinn, and Croak that he would like to show them around the grounds before they headed out on their flight. He had something incredible he thought they might like to see. Of course, they agreed.

"Oh, before I forget, Phinnius. I think you might be needing these." Ollie reached into the pocket on his plaid vest and pulled out a pair of glasses bound together in the center with twine.

Phinn jumped for joy. "My glasses! I thought these were gone forever! Where did you find them?" he asked, putting on his glasses and looking all around as if he hadn't seen the place before.

"Well, after I dropped you off with your friends yesterday, I went back to the forest and searched for your glasses. I found them on the forest floor, but unfortunately, they were broken. I'm sorry I couldn't get them to you earlier. I felt it was best for me to fix them first before returning them to you. After all, they would be of no use if they were broken." Ollie smiled.

"Thanks, Ollie!" Phinn hugged Ollie's soft belly tightly.
"You are very welcome, my friend. Now, let's be off."

The boys quickly gathered their belongings and said their good-byes to Momma before heading out. Ollie led the boys around the grounds, following the babbling brook beyond the meadow. On their way they passed the children whizzing to and fro, enjoying a game of hide-and-seek. Peanut poked her little yellow head out from behind a boulder that lay on the edge of the brook, calling out words of hello to them. Chubby's hand quickly muffled her cries, so as not to give away their location to the critter that was "it." Ribbit waved hello and put his finger to his lips, showing that their secret hiding spot was safe with him. After walking a few moments, they came to some stone stairs that crept up the side of the massive mountain behind the Enchanted Meadow. Ollie began to climb the stairs, the frogs leaping close behind.

When they reached the top of the stairs, the view took Ribbit's breath away. He was standing at the top of a roaring waterfall tumbling down the mountainside, the water creating prisms of color in the moist air. A clear blue pool formed at the base of the falls. It was edged with lush ferns and moss. A host of colorful birds delighted in the moisture as they darted and splashed playfully. In the distance, Ribbit could see the mighty oak tree and the children scampering about in the grasses below. From where he sat, he could feel the chilly mist spraying his face, awakening his senses.

"This is my favorite spot to reflect," Ollie sat down on the jagged rocks, dipping his feathers in the cold waters. "It's my meditation spot. A place where I can clear my mind, look down on my family below, and feel truly grateful for what I have."

Ribbit could understand that. Anyone would be grateful to have the life Ollie had. What's not to be grateful for? He had a loving wife, eight amazing children, a warm and cozy home, and a job that involved helping others and making a real difference. It didn't get much better than that.

"This is great, Ollie. Really great," Ribbit said, still staring below.

"This would be great, if it weren't so high!" Phinn squealed, clinging to Croak. Croak pretended like he was going to fall and stumbled nearer to the edge. Phinn shrieked and shot him a disgruntled look.

Ollie chuckled. "Alright, my little amphibians, are you ready to head out and get to the bottom of your fly dilemma?"

"You betchya!" Ribbit shouted, as he jumped up on Ollie's great spotted wings and took hold of his feathers like reigns.

"Yep! Let's get flying!" Croak called out, leaping on after Ribbit and getting his bearings on his feathery seat. "Come on, Phinn. All aboard!" He waved.

"Uhh . . . I'm not so sure about this," Phinn trembled. "My first flight was . . . how do I put this . . . terrifying!"

Ribbit had completely forgotten that Phinn had already gone for a ride on Ollie's back when he had fallen off of the cliff. In all of the excitement, it had slipped his mind that they had almost lost Phinn merely a day ago.

"Oh, come on Phinnius. No need for uncertainties. I will take good care of you—just as I did at the cliff," Ollie said reassuringly, gently scooting Phinn over to him with his giant wing.

"Why do I always let you guys talk me into these things," Phinn sighed as he shut his eyes, took in a deep breath, then hopped on Ollie's back. They all agreed he could sit in the middle since he was so nervous.

"Alright then, off we go!" Ollie sang out as he took a running start and dove off of the edge of the mountainside, soaring down the side of the waterfall before gliding gracefully above the Enchanted Meadow. Down below, the children waved good-bye and ran as far as they could, following the great owl and the three little frogs who were clinging for dear life on his back.

Ribbit had never thought about what it would be like to fly like a bird. Most of the time he feared birds because they were known to be ruthless frog-eaters. He never even took a moment to imagine what it would feel like to soar high above the ground, feeling the breeze against his skin, watching the world below as if it were a play being performed just for him. It was extraordinary! Somehow, jumping from lily pad to lily pad just wouldn't seem as thrilling after this.

Ribbit peered over Ollie's back, staring down at the tiny world below. No sign of flies yet.

The sky ahead was gloomy and gray. It was almost as if they were leaving the happy blue skies of the Enchanted Meadow and flying straight into disaster.

"How are you all faring back there?" Ollie cried out, turning his head toward the frogs. It shocked Ribbit for a moment that Ollie could turn his head completely around, but then he remembered that he had read about that in one of the books at home. Still seemed bizarre to see it, though.

"Good," they all replied in unison, their knuckles turning white from grasping onto his feathers so tightly.

"Boy, am I glad that I have these! This is a whole new experience! Way different from the first ride," Phinn said, pinching his glasses.

"Do you think we could see Lily Pad Hollow from up here?" Croak shouted.

"If the skies were a bit clearer you might," Ollie said. "But that would be diverting us from our mission, friend. We must keep an eye out for those precious flies."

The boys all nodded in agreement and began peering over Ollie's back in search of their beloved flies. It was difficult to see far down below. After many, many minutes, Ribbit's eyes began to tire. He sat up straight and closed them for a moment. Then he shook his head, rubbed his eyes, and got back to work. After all, this was no time to rest.

When he looked back down over Ollie's brown spotted wing, he saw that they were now flying over a thicket of thorny bushes. Upon closer examination, he noticed that they were moving. *Moving plants? That can't be right.* His eyes must be playing tricks on him. He closed them once more and opened them, letting them adjust. Sure enough, it still looked at if the thorny bushes were moving.

"Ollie? Are there some kind of weird bushes around here that move?" Ribbit asked, sure that Ollie would think that he was crazy.

"Are you referring to the briar patch below us, Ribbit?" Ollie cried out from up ahead.

"Yeah, they look as if they're moving or something," Ribbit added, as Phinn and Croak squished over to look down.

"I've never seen a moving bush before, Ribbit, but that doesn't mean it doesn't very well exist. Why don't we go in for a closer look?" And with that, Ollie swooped down toward the thorny briar patch. As they edged closer, they could see that it wasn't the bushes moving, but some dark objects swarming in front of the bushes.

"FLIES!!!!!" Ribbit screamed, pointing excitedly below.

"Ha ha! Good observation, Ribbit. Let's find a place for me to land so we can do a little investigating," Ollie shouted, slowly circling the area before making his final descent on a little clearing not far from the briar patch. As soon as they landed, the world seemed to get a little bit darker. Ribbit's excitement quickly vanished. They definitely were not in the Enchanted Meadow anymore.

Get Us Out of Here!

The clouds seemed to darken as they came upon a tangled wall of weathered gray branches and dead leaves. The massive thicket was knotted and twisted and covered in thorns, as if to say, "KEEP OUT!" And Ribbit wanted nothing more than to keep out. However, no matter how creepy it seemed, he had to go through it and follow those flies; the future of Lily Pad Hollow depended on it.

After much discussion, it was decided that the three frogs would head into the thicket while Ollie stayed outside as a lookout. He was much too large to make his way through the thorny branches and they needed someone to be able to warn them in case danger was near. Besides, it really was their mission, not his. He had a family depending on his safe return and Ribbit wouldn't have it any other way.

Ribbit felt small and vulnerable as they snaked their way through the thicket, the barbed branches grabbing at their ankles. The eerie silence was only broken by Phinn's constant shrieks of misery at being poked and prodded, his once crisp shorts now resembling streamers tie-dyed with dirt and blood. Although Croak didn't protest as much as Phinn, Ribbit knew that he had to be getting just as scratched up, if not more-so, due to his larger stature. After a few feet of bending and writhing, Ribbit came across a clearing in the thicket. Finally! He stepped out into the open air and let out a deep sigh, just then realizing that he had been holding his breath throughout the entire obstacle.

"Hey, guys!" Ribbit panted, peering into the dense thicket for a sign of his friends. "I found a clearing! Just a little bit farther!" he called out, inspecting his scratched limbs.

"Well, it's about time!" Phinn murmured. Ribbit could now see his scratched face through the thorns. Seeing how close he was to being out of this mess, he made a final leap into the clearing. However, in true Phinn style, his foot got stuck and he tumbled through the thicket, scratching his freckled arms even more and landing with a thud at Ribbit's feet.

"OW!"

"You always knew how to make an entrance, huh Phinny boy?" Ribbit chuckled, as he helped him to his feet and examined his scrapes. "Nothing too deep here, I think you'll live."

"Well that was no picnic!" Croak muttered, exiting the thicket, his smooth green skin etched with crimson scratches.

With everyone out safely, they began to check out their surroundings. Straight ahead, in the center of the clearing, sat a large gray boulder. From behind it, a familiar buzzing sound filled the air. Ribbit could almost smell the flies. They were getting close. As quick as the beat of a hummingbird's wing, they made their way around the giant boulder, their mouths salivating. Once on the other side, they stopped almost as abruptly as they had started. Dozens of large web-like spheres hummed in front of them, each one filled with what had to be thousands of flies, mosquitoes, and a myriad of other flying insects. A few stragglers made their way out of the bindings, frantically whizzing around and around the pods, as if devising a plan to save the others.

"Jackpot!" Croak whooped, wasting no time chasing after the escapees.

Phinn and Ribbit weren't far behind, and the three frogs frolicked around the pods, snapping their tongues and crunching on any insect that crossed their path. It was as if all their problems vanished, if only for a moment.

In his quest to catch the fattest fly he had ever seen, Phinn made his way to the far edge of the thicket before stopping in his tracks. The fat fly buzzed away to live another day. "Umm . . . guys? You need to see this." His voice shook. Ribbit and Croak stopped their feasting and quickly hopped over, smacking their lips along the way. The joy dropped from their faces as they stood staring at what looked like a prison made out of thicket branches tied together. Inside of the prison sat five large, hairy spiders.

Croak marched over, a fly wing still stuck to his lips. "Hey! Why are you spiders hogging all the flies over there? We need flies, too, you know!" he yelled, his hands firmly on his hips.

"Oh, thank goodness!" one of the spiders exclaimed. "Everyone, everyone! Get up! Someone's here to rescue us!" The spiders promptly gathered around the wall of the cage, their spindly legs dangling through the thorny bars.

"Rescue you?" Ribbit asked.

"Yes. That's what you're here for, right? Or do you want to eat us, too?" another spider asked, her eight eyes gleaming up at him.

"What in pond's name is going on here?" Phinn chimed in. "Are you spiders the ones who made these webs?"

"Well, yes. We did make the webs. But it isn't out fault! Lex made us do it," another spider chimed in, his eight arms grasping the prison bars.

"Who's Lex?" Ribbit asked.

"Lex the lizard. He's a meanie," a small spider said frantically. The other spiders looked around, as if the dreaded lizard would appear at the mention of his name. "He lives just over there, under that giant rock. He's keeping us prisoner and he said that if we don't spin these web-pods, he and his friends are going to eat us."

"No way!" Croak blurted trying his best to break the thorny branches that made up the prison cage.

"You're telling us. There were six of us . . . then Tag refused to spin," another spider said as his gaze fell to the floor. "He wanted to stand up to Lex and hold a revolt. Rest his soul." All of the spiders' heads drooped in remembrance of the fallen arachnid.

"You mean he ate him?" Ribbit looked inquiringly at the helpless spiders.

"It was a terrible sight. A terrible sight." The spider shook his head.

"GET US OUT OF HERE!" a manic spider cried out, tugging frantically on the branches of their prison with his frail legs. The memory of his fallen friend must have roused his desire to be set free so he wouldn't face the same fate.

"Wait, wait, wait!" the eldest spider called out. "Let's think a minute here. Maybe we don't want them to let us out of here." He looked suspiciously at Ribbit, Phinn, and Croak. "I mean, I've never met one before, but I do believe that these fellows are frogs."

The other spiders gasped and huddled toward the farthest corner of their prison.

"What's wrong with these guys?" Croak stuck his thumb out toward the cowering spiders.

"They think we want to eat them, algae-brain," Phinn said.

"Oh." Croak scratched his head. "*Do* we want to eat them? They are insects."

"No they're not! They're arachnids, Croak. And, somehow, seeing as these ones can talk and are showing signs of intelligence, I think not," Phinn said.

"Hey, spiders," Ribbit cried out. "There's no need to worry. We don't want to eat you."

"You don't?" the oldest spider spoke out again, stepping toward Ribbit, but holding his arm out to keep the others behind.

"No."

"But we heard that frogs like to eat spiders." The spiders all looked confused and Ribbit didn't blame them. The spiders felt about him the exact same way that he felt about Shelly and Ollie when he first met them. Now he realized how silly he must have sounded to them.

"Well, that's probably true for most frogs, but not for these frogs. We would never eat knowledgeable arachnids such as yourselves." Ribbit tried to sound as friendly and unthreatening as he could. These spiders seemed to have been through a lot of fear and pain already, and the last thing he wanted to do was make them feel worse. "So, if it's alright with you, we're gonna try to set you free."

The spiders huddled together, whispering and debating whether or not to trust the strange little frogs that stood before them. After a minute of deliberation, they made a decision. They figured since they already had a fierce lizard threatening to gobble them up, what could these three frogs do that was much worse?

The three frogs quickly got to work. They tried their best to avoid the sharp thorns and reach for the smooth branches, but it was nearly impossible not to get pricked when they were using all their strength to free the spiders. Finally, after minutes of stretching and tearing and yanking (and bleeding), the frogs were able to make a large enough opening for the spiders to slip through.

"We're free! Thank you! Thank you! Thank you!" the spiders cried out as they scurried into the dense thicket and disappeared from sight. Only the oldest spider lingered behind.

"I knew we made a good decision trusting you frogs," he said, smiling up at his rescuers. "I'll be sure to spread the word of your good deed across the land. And if there's anything that you need from us spiders, all you have to do is ask." He gave a slight bow before scampering off after his companions.

Ribbit felt good about saving the spiders, even if he had surrendered his hands to the mercy of the briar patch. It was the first time that he actually felt like he had made a difference on this journey. It also gave him the information that he was looking for. Lex was the one who was taking all of the flies and Ribbit knew what had to be done.

Down We Go!

"Alright, guys. Let's go check out that boulder and see if we can find Lex," Ribbit called out as he bounded over to the giant boulder sitting in the center of the clearing.

"Oh, no you don't!" Phinn squealed, pointing his finger high in the air. "You're crazy if you think I'm going anywhere near that maniac!"

"Phinn, we traveled all this way. Don't you want to find out the truth about what's happening?" Ribbit asked. There was no way he was going to turn around and go home after everything they'd done to get here. He wanted answers and he was going to get them, even if it meant doing something that he really didn't want to do.

"Oh yeah, sure. Let's just go and taunt this evil lizard we know absolutely nothing about, other than his name and that he has been known to kill if provoked, to find out his dastardly plan. Good idea,

Ribbit," Phinn sneered. Ribbit didn't appreciate his sarcasm. Not at a time like this when something so important was on the line.

Croak stood silently watching the two of them bicker, his eyes shifting between Ribbit and Phinn as they each spoke their piece. He found that when Ribbit and Phinn got to arguing, it was best for him to stay out of it until they reached a conclusion.

"Alright then, Phinn. You can just stay out here if you want to, but I'm gonna check things out. After all, that's what I'm here for in the first place and I'm not going home until I find out what is going on, even if that means I have to face some evil lizard."

Irritated and fuming, Ribbit leapt over to the boulder and inspected its base until he found a small, dark opening at the far end. It was a tunnel leading down below to who knows what. Ignoring the voice in his head shrieking, *Don't do it!*, he crouched down, squinted his eyes, and peered into the darkness. At first, there seemed to be nothing but the black. But suddenly, a flicker of light caught his eye.

"Hey, guys! I think there's something down here!" Ribbit yelled, inching closer to the quivering light, his voice echoing all around him. He extended his body into the tunnel as far as he possibly could, his smooth skin stretched taught like a rubber band that could snap at any moment. Without warning, the dirt under his hand gave way and before he knew it, he was hurled forward as the darkness swallowed him up.

He landed with a thud. Chilled to the bone and achy all over, he pulled himself up and tried to get his bearings, his eyes adjusting to the dimness. He inhaled the musky air, feeling it coat his lungs with its thick, clammy texture—a far cry from the refreshing, sweet smelling aroma of the Enchanted Meadow. From what he could see, he had tumbled down into a cavern that wound underground like a dark, foreboding maze. An eerie fog hugged the ground, creeping and curling along the rock formations. All around him, water trickled down the rough rocky walls and dripped from the giant stalactites that hung from the cavern ceiling. Small torches lit up the cave, their flames dancing and glistening on the wet walls. The sound of wings flapping in the distance accompanied by a high-pitched twittering sound suggested the presence of bats. *Ugh . . . bats.* He trembled at the thought of the creepy, flying mammals he had read about in R.T. Hopkins' stories. Just imagining their leathery wings and beady eyes always sent shivers down Ribbit's spine. Through all the twittering, he could also hear the sound of voices in the distance. Deep, menacing voices that echoed throughout the walls of the cavern. Ribbit knew it had to be Lex and his comrades. He had to get closer, had to hear what they were saying.

He grabbed a torch from the wall and began to make his way through the mud puddles and toward the voices when he was distracted by a thunderous crashing sound, followed by high-pitched whines. Ribbit turned around so abruptly that he nearly fell over.

"Get off of me!" Phinn wheezed, his scraggly arms and legs flying every which way. Croak looked dazed as he rolled off of Phinn. Ribbit was so relieved to see his buddies that he wanted to scream with joy, but he had to keep his guard up—danger was near.

"Whoa! Check out this place," Croak gasped, looking around.

"Okay, okay. You've got me here. You happy now, Ribbit?" Phinn muttered as he stood up, trying to brush the dirt off of his face and arms.

"SHHHH!" Ribbit hissed. "Listen."

Phinn's eyes bulged out in fear, as Croak let out a loud gulp. The look of wonder swiftly disappeared from their faces. They could hear the voices, too.

"That's got to be Lex and his buddies. Grab a torch from the wall and let's go see if we can hear what they're saying," Ribbit instructed. He turned toward the voices and crept down the long corridor of the cave.

"Uh, you sure this is a good idea, Ribbit? Couldn't we just turn around, find a way back up to the surface, and let the flies go without dealing with this maniac?" Phinn hesitated, his voice trembling.

"Yes, and all of the flies would return to Lily Pad Hollow. Problem solved, right?" Ribbit asked.

"Right," Croak nodded, turning around toward the entrance.

"Wrong, guys!" Ribbit grabbed a hold of Croak's vest, jerking him back to where they were standing. "There's a reason he's trying to take all of the flies away from everyone. If we just let the flies go, what's to say he won't just kidnap some more spiders and do this all over again?"

Phinn and Croak stared silently back at Ribbit.

"We just need to get a little closer to hear what they're saying. Maybe they'll say something about why they're trapping all of the flies. Then maybe we can figure out a way to stop them," Ribbit said convincingly. "Oh and Phinn?" he whispered, turning to face his friends. "To answer your question: Yes, I'm happy you're here, regardless of the circumstances."

A smile danced across Phinn's face. Then, with a deep "what am I getting myself into" sigh, Croak and Phinn each grabbed a torch from the wall and prepared to follow their friend toward the unexpected.

Lex's Lair

As they made their way through the dark cavern tunnels, the echoing voices sounded closer and closer. Ribbit's hand began to tremble and moisten with sweat as he clutched his torch in front of him, using it as both a flashlight and a possible weapon if Lex or one of his accomplices happened to turn the corner. For a moment, his mind drifted as he wondered how it had come to this. Less than a week ago, he sat by the water's edge in Lily Pad Hollow, slurping down a mosquito milkshake, laughing with his friends as usual. Now, he was in the lair of the most evil, conniving creature he would ever encounter. If someone had told Ribbit a week ago that he would be here, doing this, he would have laughed in their face. He would have said something along the lines of, "I wish I could meet an evil foe like that! I'd show him what I'm made of!" And he would have been totally clueless of how it really felt. This was definitely no imaginary battle. The villain and the danger were real—very real.

It was so eerily quiet in the caverns that Ribbit thought he could hear Lex creeping up behind him and feel his breath on the back of his neck. Maybe it was the distant twittering of bats or the constant trickle of water down the cavern walls. Maybe it was the sound of his imagination, his fears getting the best of him. He couldn't be sure, but he had to go on.

Please, please, please don't let him be there! Ribbit thought to himself as he rounded every corner. He had no idea what he would do if he was confronted by Lex. He hadn't really thought that far ahead.

His pulse quickened, his adrenaline pumping so fast that although he had been walking for quite some time, he felt like it was only seconds before they were at the opening to a room. He was almost walking on autopilot, his feet leading the way while his brain remained shut down. Ribbit motioned to Phinn and Croak that they had made it to Lex's lair. Phinn and Croak immediately caught on, pressing their bodies tightly on the walls of the cavern, not moving, not breathing. Ribbit did the same. His breathing never sounded so loud, as it always does when you're trying to hide. He wished that he didn't have to breathe. That he could hold his breath for minutes at a time and be completely silent, as if he were swimming underwater. He was sure that the lizards would hear his frightened panting and come in for an attack. Luckily, no such thing happened.

Gathering up all of his courage, he slowly crept toward the entrance of the lair, holding his breath and imagining that he was one with the wall. Then he leaned slightly into the chamber, just enough to see what these terrible lizards looked like.

Inside the torch-lit chamber, three lizards sat on jagged stalagmites, dealing cards and playing a poker game. Ribbit had expected Lex to be big, brawny, intimidating, and ugly. He imagined him to be a stereotypical bad guy whose appearance just screamed evil. So when he looked into the room and saw the three lizards, he was pretty sure he knew which one was Lex.

One of the lizards was wearing a bandana and smoking a cigar. Along his cheek was a giant scar. He had a shrill voice that was meant for scheming and plotting. Upon first look, Ribbit knew he couldn't be Lex. The lizard's eyes shifted as if he were unsure— not confident and stately as he expected Lex to be.

Across from him sat another lizard who was missing a front tooth and had scars and scratches all over his thick, burly arms. His voice was deep and grumbly, what you would expect a bad guy to sound like. It sent shivers down Ribbit's spine. That must have been the voice that Ribbit could hear echoing in the cavern tunnels on his way here. He seemed to be the largest (and ugliest) of the three. He had to be Lex. Ribbit was sure of it.

The third lizard was very different from the other two. Although his back was toward Ribbit, he was clearly the smallest of the three lizards and his voice didn't have the same dark tone to it as the other two. It seemed more smooth and even. *Who was this guy?*

The more he spoke, the more familiar he began to sound to Ribbit. *Where had he heard that voice before?* It couldn't have been at Lily Pad Hollow because there were no lizards that lived around there, so it had to be someone that he met on his journey. Had to be someone from either the Turtle house or . . .

Suddenly, it hit him like a bolt of lightening. It was Alexander.

The more he spoke, the more Ribbit was sure of it. But what was he doing with those scumbags? Was he being held captive or something? He had to be. Why else would he be there with those two thugs? Alexander was way too nice of a lizard to be friends with those guys voluntarily. Something was up.

Ribbit slowly leaned back out of the doorway and hugged tightly to the slick wall as he crept back toward Phinn and Croak. They were both squirming with anxiousness.

"So? So? What'd you see?" Phinn whispered, his eyes bulging.

"Alexander's in there."

"Who?" asked Croak.

"You know! The lizard from Shelly's house. He's in there with two mean-looking lizards. They must be holding him hostage or something." Ribbit said. His friends were stunned in silence. "I'm gonna take another look and see if I can hear what they're saying. Maybe we can get to the bottom of this and figure out a way to get Alexander out of there." Phinn and Croak looked at each other, but before they could utter a word, Ribbit was gone.

Slowly, slowly, slowly, Ribbit made his way back toward the lair. Once again, he leaned his body, ever so slightly, into the doorway to listen. He could see that the lizards were still playing their cards and hadn't heard him creep up on them.

He strained his ears to listen carefully.

"I'll see your two diamonds and raise you two more amethysts," the lizard wearing the bandana muttered, his cigar clenched tightly between his teeth. Then, showing no emotion and staring directly in his opponents' eyes, he pushed forward his gems that twinkled in the torchlight.

"Oh, I see, Canker. You wanna play with the big boys," the largest lizard groaned, pushing his gems forward and spitting to his left side. "Alright, I'll see your two amethysts and raise you three emeralds. Boo-yah! How's that, pretty boy?"

"Pretty boy? Pretty boy? Who you callin' pretty boy, fatso!" Canker roared, pushing his chair back and standing up in confrontation.

"Now, now, now, fellas. No need to be hostile." Alexander spoke out, his smooth voice polishing the air. "Have a seat, Canker. And you, Boomer, play nice."

Boomer? Boomer? I thought he was Lex! Ribbit thought to himself. *Well, if he isn't Lex . . .*

Realization slapped Ribbit in the face, jolting his heart and sucking the breath right out of him.

Of course! Lex *is short for* Alexander*!! A-LEX-ander.*

Ribbit was sure that when he came across the evil foe responsible for stealing all of the flies that he would see through him in an instant. But Lex had fooled him, had fooled the Turtle family for years, and was probably fooling everyone.

"Sorry, boss. It won't happen again," Canker grumbled, returning to his seat and to smoking his cigar.

"Yeah, sorry, Lex," Boomer said shyly, now resembling more of a boy than a terrifying lizard.

The three lizards continued their poker game and Ribbit carefully ducked out of the doorway, his mind in a flurry, and scurried back to his buddies. He was about to drop the biggest surprise on them that they would ever hear.

*****

"Whoa, whoa, whoa! So, Lex is Alexander?" Croak said.

"Yes! He's Lex! I heard it with my own ears. The other two are Canker and Boomer. They do everything Lex tells them to."

"Nice names," Phinn snorted with a smile.

"Trust me, when you see them it will all make sense," Ribbit said.

Phinn's smile quickly dropped.

"No way!" Croak said loudly. Phinn quickly covered Croak's mouth with his hand, so no other words could escape. Croak swatted Phinn's hand and shot him an angry look.

"Don't look at me like, that. Your loud mouth's gonna get us eaten by those lizards." Phinn began pacing back and forth, mumbling to himself. "This can't be happening! This can't be happening! This has to be a nightmare. There's no way that I'm actually here in this dark, scary cave with these horrific lizards sitting just feet away. It has to be a nightmare," Phinn repeated, nodding eagerly as if convincing himself that it was true.

Croak grabbed Phinn by the shoulders and slapped him across the face. "Pull yourself together, frog."

"Hey!" Phinn looked sorely at Croak. "Was that really necessary?"

"Yep. You were losing it," Croak responded dryly.

Phinn shook his head, as if he were trying to shake off a bad memory, adjusted his glasses, and took a deep breath, signaling that he had, in fact, pulled himself together.

"So, what now?" Croak asked, looking at Ribbit for an answer.

"I think I have a plan that just might work," Ribbit said, gathering his friends in a huddle. "I'm gonna go around the chamber to the opening in the back and see if I can hear any more of what they're talking about. Croak, I want you to go to the entrance over there." Ribbit pointed to where he had just come from. "All you're gonna do is listen and see what you can find out. Got it?"

"Yep," Croak nodded.

Ribbit nodded back and turned to Phinn. "Phinn, I want you to head back where we came in and see if there's a way for us to get out of here quickly. Once we get the information we need, Croak and I will come and meet you at the entrance."

"I'm good with that. The sooner we can get outta here, the better!" Phinn gulped.

*****

"Full house! Read 'em and weep, boys. Time to pay up!" Lex gloated, laying down his winning cards and gathering all of the gems with his rough, scaly arms.

"Good one, boss!" Boomer boomed.

"Yeah, good one, boss," Canker repeated.

"Nice try, fellas. Maybe next time." Lex smiled, counting his bounty and stashing it in a satchel that was slung around his chair. "Ugh . . ." he sighed. "What a day." He put his feet up on the table to rest.

"Yeah, boss. We finally caught that old turtle and made him pay up," Boomer smirked.

"Careful, now," Lex insisted forcefully. "Otis is an old friend. It's just too bad that he couldn't hold up his end of the bargain."

Ribbit's heart leapt into his throat. They had Mr. Turtle.

"I really thought that he would be able to scrounge up eight spiders with no problem. Really, was it too much to ask for? I've been providing his family with flies for weeks now and all he had to do was get me eight lousy spiders. Is that so ridiculous?" Lex pleaded, fully knowing that his companions would tell him what he wanted to hear.

"Of course not, boss. It was very generous of you," Canker sniveled.

"I know it was," Lex exhaled. "Still, it's just a shame that it had to be this way. But, he knew the consequences when he made the deal. No spiders, no freedom. I held up my end of the bargain and he failed to hold up his. What a pity."

"He deserved it, Boss" Boomer encouraged, nodding his head.

"Well, at least we caught him before he made it home. We don't want anyone else catching on. Not that I'm too worried about Myrtle figuring it out. And it's laughable that those little frogs staying with her actually think that they're gonna figure out what's going on with the flies."

All three of them shared a devious chuckle.

"Childhood ambition, I guess." He looked down at his claws, picking at them and polishing them on his shirt. "The good news is, gentlelizards, that our plan is working." His mouth twisted into a sinister smile as he looked at Canker and Boomer. "I don't recall exactly where they said they came from, but I do know that it was far away. That can only mean that the flies are beginning to dwindle even outside our area." He sucked in a deep, satisfied breath. "And those little frogs are just gonna have to join the ranks of creatures begging me and making deals just to have a taste of their precious flies. It's going to be magnificent: all of those creatures at my mercy. It's only a matter of time."

So there it was, the answer to all of Ribbit's questions. He thought that once he had the answer, the solution would be clear. He thought that finding out the reason for the missing flies would somehow lead him to a way to put an end to the madness. However, now that he was here—now that he could practically feel the warm breath of his enemy—his mind went completely blank. He had nothing.

For the first time during his adventure, Ribbit felt hopeless. How was he, a little frog from a small pond, going to stop this conniving mastermind? There was clearly no reasoning with Lex. If his plan succeeded, soon enough every creature would bow to him and offer him whatever they had to get their beloved flies back. He would be their ruler and their king. It was a brilliant plan, a devilishly brilliant plan.

Ribbit slunk away from the opening and back into the dim tunnel. He let his tired body fall to the floor, resting his back against the damp wall. For a moment, he stared into space, his mind blank, his heart heavy. Then he realized that if he just gave up, if he just left and did nothing, he would be no better than Canker or Boomer. He would be aiding Lex's plan by being passive and watching it happen.

That thought was just the motivation he needed to get his brain ticking again. He shot back up to his feet and came up with an idea: as much as he didn't want to, he would have to physically stop Lex from carrying out his plans.

Ribbit could hear his heart pounding in his ears. He knew what had to be done. He had been training for this moment his entire life, practicing with reeds and cattails, preparing himself for battle. Now, his moment had come. He set down his pack, gripped his torch as his mighty sword, closed his eyes, and took a deep breath. He stopped abruptly as Croak's voice rang in his ears.

Ribbit peered into the chamber once more and saw Croak inside, standing face to face with Lex.

The Capture

"Hey," Croak announced, standing up straight and staring the three lizards in the eyes. "We know what you're doin' and we aren't gonna let you get away with it."

"Well, looky here!" Lex's face twisted into a sinister reptilian smile. He looked at Croak so menacingly that Ribbit almost stopped breathing. "I guess I underestimated you, little frog."

"You bet you did. Now, you're coming with me," Croak said, speaking to Lex in the same firm tone that he often used with Squiggy and Kilroy.

The three lizards roared with laughter.

"Okay, okay!" Lex giggled mockingly, his arms raised in surrender. "You got me! You got me!"

Ribbit knew that Lex was being sarcastic, but unfortunately, as usual, his naive buddy wasn't catching on.

"I'm glad you aren't going to fight me on this one,

Alexander, or should I call you, Lex!" Croak snapped, his hands firmly on his hips.

"Ah, someone's been eavesdropping, has he?" Lex hissed, his once friendly tone infected with wickedness.

"You bet we have," Croak replied indignantly.

"*We*, you say?" Lex sneered, his demonic face lit with curiosity. "So, where are your little friends anyway?"

"That's none of your business, Lex. I'm taking you in. Now, I don't want this to get ugly. So let's just head out of here and we'll tell everyone the truth. The jig is up." Croak grabbed Lex's arm in an attempt to lead him out of the cavern.

Lex sniggered, shooting a venomous grin at Canker and Boomer. "Alright, enough of this nonsense. Get him," he commanded sharply, as Canker and Boomer roughly seized Croak's arms in an iron grasp from behind.

Croak fought back, kicking and struggling to free himself, but it was no use. Canker and Boomer's strength overpowered his own.

"What shall we do with him, boss?" Canker sniveled in a cold, cruel voice as he held Croak's wriggling arm tightly.

"Put him in with Otis," Lex ordered, a splinter of ice in his voice. He dismissed them with a wave of his hand as he turned his back and began to gather up his jewels. "I'll go find those other irritating frogs and handle them myself."

Ribbit stood frozen, feeling as if the slightest touch might knock him over. It seemed almost like a dream, like a nightmare. He had to stop them from taking Croak away, but he was too terrified to move. These lizards were dangerous; nothing like Kilroy and Squiggy, as Croak just found out. They meant harm on a different level and were capable of terrible things. Ribbit was in way over his head and couldn't find the strength to do anything.

Then, it happened.

His eyes met with Croak's and his heart broke. He was watching his best friend, his buddy, being carted away to his doom. Was he really going to do nothing? Looking into Croak's frightened eyes gave Ribbit the jolt he needed. There was no way he was just going to stand there and let this happen, no matter the consequences.

Ribbit clutched his torch, feeling the warmth radiate from its fiery tip. Taking in a big gulp of air and ignoring the fear that prickled in his spine, he sprang out from behind the opening and, using his torch in the same way that he had always used his reeds, he plunged at Boomer, stabbing the fiery torch into his leathery skin. Boomer let out a howl, releasing Croak from his grip and flailing his arms in an attempt to brush the burn off his singed back.

The torch's once blazing fire was put out from the attack on Boomer, but the tip glowed red, warning that it was still searing hot.

"What's wrong with you?" Canker called out to Boomer. Luckily for Ribbit, Boomer's burly body blocked Ribbit from Canker's view, keeping him safe for the moment.

He knew he had to act fast, so Ribbit popped out from behind Boomer and quickly swung his torch again. This time the torch made contact with Canker's head, knocking him unconscious, his body falling hard on the cavern floor.

"RUN, CROAK!" Ribbit yelped.

Croak did as he was told and bounded out of there as fast as his froggy legs would allow.

"Get him!" Lex barked at Boomer. Although Boomer's back was badly burned, exposing a raw, pink spot, he ran down the corridor after Croak.

Ribbit stared at Lex's cold, steely eyes—black as night. *What have I done?* He was now in the belly of the monster and there was no turning back. Ribbit wished that he could go back in time, let the spiders free, break down the pods, and get the heck out of here. Why had he insisted on going down into this cavern?

He stood motionless, his knees like jelly, every inch of his being telling him to run. Yet, his feet remained planted, the torch pointing at a seething Lex. Acting like a hero wasn't as fun as Ribbit thought it would be. He didn't feel brave. In fact, he was now more afraid than ever.

"Big mistake, Ribbit!" Lex growled, baring pointy teeth.

"How could you? They trusted you." Ribbit struggled to keep his voice steady. "We trusted you."

Lex shot him a withering look. "By 'they' you mean the Turtle family, right?"

Ribbit nodded. His throat was dry and tight.

"Yes, well, it's unfortunate that things have to be this way. I really do like the Turtle family. They have been friends of mine for years . . ."

"Friends!" Ribbit screeched. "You're no friend of theirs!"

"Oh, Ribbit. You are so young and there is so much that you don't understand. Yes, the Turtles are my friends. Otis was their downfall."

"What do you mean?" Ribbit's voice trembled.

"He made a deal," Lex muttered crossly. His nostrils flared like an angry bull. "I didn't want to involve my friends in my plans. But he's the one who made it happen this way."

"What are you talking about?" Ribbit couldn't understand what Lex was saying. He didn't know Mr. Turtle at all, but he found it hard to believe that Shelly's dad would put their family in jeopardy. It just didn't seem like something a responsible, caring father would do. Then again, Ribbit couldn't be sure.

"It's those accursed animals in town. This is all their fault," Lex seethed, a distant expression on his face. "You know what really got to me, Ribbit? Everyone's attitudes toward us lizards. To them, we are either mindless reptiles who scurry under rocks in the face of danger, or we are lazy creatures who like to sun ourselves, completely useless to animal kind. In fact, I bet you never even thought twice about us lizards, have you Ribbit?"

"Well, I never met one before—"

"No, why would you!" Lex interrupted, dismissing Ribbit's response. He threw his hands wildly in the air and continued his ranting. "We're of no importance to the high society of animals who build and hunt and forage. Not like our snake cousins who strike fear into the hearts of all those who encounter them, or turtles who educate themselves and pass knowledge through their words. No, no, no, no, no!" Lex shook his head furiously. "We are pitiful, worthless, reptiles, right? Meant to snivel and stand in awe of others' achievements, while having nothing of our own?"

Ribbit fell silent as if he had just swallowed his tongue. He dared not answer, for he knew that Lex wasn't seeking a response. Besides, he didn't even have a clue about what to say. He had been blissfully unaware that these sort of problems, or that these types of animals, existed at all.

"Well, not anymore. From now on, we'll get the respect we deserve." Lex's face split into an amused, demonic grin. "They'll regret the day that they dismissed us and they'll pay for their ignorant ways when I'm in charge of their food—their very lives will be in my hands." He held out his palms, admiring them as if they were made of gold.

"I get it. I really do. You want to be treated fairly," Ribbit agreed, afraid that if he spoke a word of protest that Lex would channel that fury he was feeling over his injustice toward him. "But, where does Mr. Turtle fit into all of this?"

"It was never my intention for Otis to get involved," Lex answered. "You see, he was one of the few creatures that actually treated me like an equal. But one day, he came to me talking about how much his family was going to hurt without flies. He had no idea what I was up to, of course, but he knew that I had a way of finding flies. So, we made a deal. I assured him that I'd give his family all the flies they needed, so long as he provided me with eight large spiders. That was it. No strings attached." Lex stared unblinking at the ground, seeming genuinely upset by the whole thing. "However," he continued, his beady eyes now fixed on Ribbit, "Otis didn't do as he promised. I had no choice. I'd been providing his family with countless flies and he was not holding up his end of the bargain. When I discussed it with him, he acted as if he were giving up, as if he had provided me with enough spiders and I should just let it go. I was not about to let that old turtle walk all over me like the others."

Ribbit was surprised that Lex was divulging all of this information to him instead of just tearing him to bits with his razor-sharp teeth and claws. Maybe he just wanted someone to talk to, beside Canker and Boomer. Maybe saying it out loud just made him feel better. Whatever the reason, Ribbit wanted answers, so he went on. "What are you gonna do with him?" he asked, not sure if he wanted to hear the truth.

As if he were reading Ribbit's thoughts, Lex's mood changed quicker than the snap of a mousetrap. His inky eyes seared into Ribbit's in a feverish rage. "That's no concern of yours, now is it, Ribbit?"

Ribbit couldn't hold it in any longer. He had to tell Lex what he thought of him, no matter the consequences. "You're a monster!" Ribbit lashed out, his body trembling with fury. "You're nothing more than a coward, Lex! A coward who can't stand up for himself so he has to terrorize everyone without even showing his face!"

"A coward? A coward?" Lex repeated through clenched teeth. "Do you have any idea who you're talking to?" He inched closer to Ribbit and stared at him so penetratingly that Ribbit half expected his gaze to scorch a hole right through him.

Ribbit squeezed his torch so hard his fingers hurt. It was all he could do to stand there and stare back into Lex's unrelenting eyes. It felt good to say those words, but he knew that he was in for a world of hurt and he was no match for Lex's size and power. Just when Ribbit expected Lex to attack, Lex's gaze shifted to something above Ribbit's head. Ribbit didn't dare turn around. He didn't know what was behind him, but he couldn't risk turning his back on Lex. Whatever it was, it couldn't be more dangerous than the ticking time bomb before him.

Lex's mouth curled up into a snarled smile, an evil gleam in his eye. It chilled Ribbit to the bone. No one had ever looked at Ribbit like that before.

"Nighty night, little frog," he hissed, waving his leathery hand.

Before Ribbit could respond, he was struck with a hard blow. He felt his knees buckle and his body hit the floor hard. The room went dark.

It Can't End This Way

Ribbit opened his eyes. The room was a blur, not that there was much to see. He was enveloped in darkness, but he could tell that he was in a small area and he suspected, by the lack of any natural light, that he was still in the cavern somewhere. Emptiness oozed from the walls around him. How did he get here?

His head throbbed. He put his hand up to it and felt a lump the size of his fist. Maybe his attack on Canker hadn't been as fatal as he had originally thought. He must have awoken while Ribbit was talking to Lex and attacked him from behind. It was the only explanation that made any sense.

A rustling sound to his right quickly snapped him out of his haze, his senses acute and ready for action.

"Who's there?" His voice came out squeakier than he would have liked. He wanted to sound threatening and dangerous to whomever was in the room with him, not like a defenseless, tiny cricket.

"Oh, relax, little one. I'm a prisoner just like you. I mean you no harm," a dry, somber voice said aloud.

Although his mind was still cloudy, Ribbit remembered that Lex was holding Mr. Turtle captive. It had to be his voice that Ribbit was hearing. "Mr. Turtle?" he called out into the darkness, his eyes squinting in an attempt to distinguish the shape of his fellow prisoner. "Is that you?"

"As a matter of fact, it is. And who might you be?" asked Otis Turtle, sounding very confused.

Ribbit released a heartfelt sigh. "Uh . . . my name is Ribbit. I'm a friend of Shelly's. I stayed with your family a few nights ago. They sort of saved our lives. And they were kind enough to take in me and my friends when we had nowhere to stay."

"Sounds like my Myrtle and Shelly." He sat quietly for a moment before continuing. "Well then, Ribbit, it's nice to meet you, although I wish it could've been under different circumstances." Ribbit could hear the scratching of Otis's claws on the rough dirt floor as he stepped closer. Even through the darkness, Ribbit could sense that they were standing right beside each other.

"Where are we?" Ribbit asked, swinging his arms in the blackness to try and touch whatever he could. All he could feel was solid rock.

"Unfortunately, we're in some sort of a hole, Ribbit. I've been here for a few days, I think. Kind of hard to tell when you can't see the sun." He heaved a deep, defeated sigh. "I've tried everything I could to get out of here, but it's just no use. I fear that we're pretty deep down."

Ribbit wasn't about to let that stop him from trying to climb up the walls, grasping on to any uneven surface he could find. He wished that he had longer legs, longer arms, longer everything! He scrambled and clawed and stretched, but Otis was right, it was no use.

"I hate to say I told you so," Otis said softly, like a feathery whisper.

Tears began to well in Ribbit's eyes. His lips began to tremble and there was nothing he could do about it. He was trapped. Hopelessly and utterly trapped. He slumped against the cold wall and let his body slide to the floor. He sat with his lean arms wrapped around his legs, resting his chin on his knees, feeling the cold tears trickle down his face. His future looked bleak. He was officially giving up.

Otis sensed Ribbit's discouragement and tried his best to comfort him. "There, there." He slid his arm gently around Ribbit's back. "No need to fret. This is just a temporary setback. This isn't how our story ends, Ribbit."

"How do you know?" Ribbit sniffled.

"I just know. Can't you just feel it? This isn't how it ends. Not like this."

Ribbit shut his eyes and listened to his gut. Otis was right. Every last fiber of his being told him that this was not the end. He could have imagined his end when he stood in front of Lex, taunting the madman and challenging him to a fight. But now, in this strange hole far below ground with no enemy in sight, this was definitely not going to be his end.

Ribbit wiped off his tears and sat up straight. How was it that a simple sentence could change his feelings so drastically? He went from feeling hopeless, to feeling hopeful with a matter of words. "I feel it, too," he said. "So, what do we do now?"

"We wait," Otis replied. "We have good people around us, Ribbit, who won't just sit back and let this happen. We have to have faith that they will come to our aide. It's really our only hope."

"So, we just sit here and do nothing?" Ribbit asked, his body twitching with the need to do something rather than simply wait to be rescued. It had never been like Ribbit to sit around and wait for someone else to do the dirty work. He never imagined his great conquest to be like this.

"Now, I didn't say that. We have only one weapon down here." Otis paused. Silence once again filled the air with its heavy sighs.

Ribbit squinted through the darkness, desperately searching for what Otis could be talking about. What could he have missed? He scanned through the darkness and found what he had suspected: there were no weapons. There was only a small frog and an old turtle.

"What are you talking about?" he finally blurted. He was

beginning to think that maybe Otis had been down in this hole for a little too long.

"You don't get it do you, Ribbit. We have the most powerful weapon down here. More powerful than what those goons up there have."

Ribbit wasn't sure how to respond, so he didn't.

"I'm referring to our minds, Ribbit. Our minds are our greatest weapon."

"Our minds? What do you mean?" Ribbit asked, hoping that Otis' answer wouldn't sound as crazy as Ribbit was guessing it would. The last thing he needed right now was to be stuck with a crazy, old turtle.

Otis gently knocked on Ribbit's head. "Ribbit, things are too black and white in that little head of yours. Think about it for a moment. No, I don't mean that our minds are literally weapons that can physically destroy Lex. I'm not that daft."

Ribbit could feel his cheeks turn red. He was glad that it was too dark for Otis to see him.

"What I mean is that it's not going to be a difficult task to outsmart those bozos. The mind can be a powerful thing, Ribbit, when used in the right manner."

Ribbit knew he was right. They were going to have to work together to outsmart those evil lizards if they ever wanted to see the light of day again.

*****

Inside the dark corridors of the cavern, Croak leapt for his life. He was bounding around each corner, desperately searching for Phinn and a way out. He could hear Boomer trailing not far behind him, but his thoughts were more focused on Ribbit. Ribbit had saved him. He had given up his own life, his own safety for his. He didn't even want to think about what had happened to him. It made his stomach curl at the possibilities of what Lex was capable of. All he could do was have faith that Ribbit was a crafty frog. His only job now was to get himself to safety where he could go for help. *I'm coming back for you, Ribbit,* he thought. *Just hold on, buddy.*

As he turned the corner, he bumped hard into something—actually, someone. His heart stopped and he braced himself for the worst. But then, he heard a familiar squeal.

"Phinn!" Croak yelped, happy to see his scrawny friend.

"Ow! Well that's a fine greeting," Phinn said, picking himself up. "Where's Ribbit?"

Croak looked down. He knew he couldn't tell Phinn what had just happened without Phinn having a total meltdown. He was going to have to quickly change the subject and get them out of there. "He'll be along soon," he lied. "Did you find a way out?"

"Are you kidding? You think I'd still be in this awful place if I had?" Phinn picked up his spectacles, which had fallen off in the collision. They had a small scratch, but were still usable.

"Ugh," Croak grunted. "Where should we go?"

"Well, if my memory serves me, we came in from that direction, I think," Phinn said, pointing down another long corridor, lined with torches flickering on the wall. Just then, they could hear Boomer's grunts echoing in the distance.

"Are they coming for us? Tell me they aren't coming for us, Croak!" Phinn shrieked.

"Uh . . . they aren't coming for us," Croak repeated unconvincingly. There was no time to work on his acting right now. He was having a hard enough time not spilling the news about Ribbit.

Phinn opened his mouth to reply, but Croak quickly shoved his hand over his mouth before a single sound could come out. "Phinn . . . take us to the entrance. Now!" With that, the two frogs disappeared into the darkness.

*****

Ribbit sat on the hard floor, fiddling with a rock he had found on the ground. More than anything he wished for his pack so he could light up his firefly nightlight and be swept away from reality by one of R.T. Hopkins' fantastic tales. *What happened to my pack?* he wondered. He knew he had it on when he entered the cavern, but he wasn't sure if he had it on during the attack. No, in fact, he distinctly remembered taking it off just before Croak was captured, so it had to be in the cavern somewhere. He hoped Lex hadn't found it and discarded his precious books.

"So, what's the plan?" Ribbit asked into the darkness.

"Well, I've had a lot of time down here to sit and think about Lex's weaknesses. I came up with one piece of information that I think may be useful to us," Otis said.

Ribbit set down his rock and leaned in closer toward Otis. In the darkness, he could almost make out his wrinkled face. He looked tired, but Ribbit could see a spark of determination in his eyes.

"Lex is deathly afraid of birds, so if we could find a way to make a pretend bird or—"

Ribbit's heart skipped a beat. "That's perfect!" he interrupted, standing up in his excitement.

"What? What's perfect?" Otis sputtered.

"I came here on an owl." Ribbit beamed, a smile overtaking his face.

"An owl? I don't quite understand. Was he hunting you?" Otis asked.

"No, it's nothing like that." Ribbit couldn't help but giggle. "He's a nice owl who's helping us find out what happened to all of the flies. He's on our side," Ribbit cried out cheerfully.

"Do you think he'll help us get rid of Lex?"

"Absolutely!"

"Well that's great news!" Otis exclaimed, standing up. "That will be perfect! If we can get Lex outside of his cavern, then we can scare the daylights out of him with your owl friend."

Ribbit felt excitement jolt throughout his body. This plan could actually work.

"So, what do we do?" Ribbit said, once again feeling antsy to get to work and start acting on something.

"Well, we could start mapping out a plan, but I'm afraid it is too dark down here. We won't be able to see what we are doing." Otis began to shuffle around. Ribbit felt like he should do the same, even though he wasn't quite sure what they were doing.

"What are we looking for?" Ribbit asked.

"Rocks and a stick," Otis answered.

"And why are we looking for that?"

"To make a fire. I can rub the two rocks together to make a spark that will ignite the stick. Help me." Ribbit should have known that Mr. Turtle would come up with such an ingenious plan; he was a turtle after all.

Ribbit reached for the rock that he was just fiddling with and found it exactly where he had left it.

"Got one rock!" His voice echoed in the darkness.

"Great! I found one over here as well. Now, if we could just find something flammable like a stick or a piece of wood or paper," Otis said.

Again, if only Ribbit had his pack. Then they could have lit up his firefly nightlight and got to planning already. He shook his head. It was no use thinking that way.

Ribbit reached his hands around, touching and feeling every inch of the hole. As he worked his way up the side of the rocky wall, he felt something protruding. It felt hard, like a rock, but Ribbit could tell by the texture that it wasn't. No, the texture of this thing felt different. He used his finger to claw at it and he felt its top layer peel off under his fingers. Whatever it was, it was made of wood. Ribbit was sure of that.

"I found something, Mr. Turtle! I found something!" Ribbit shrieked. "Come here! Come here!"

Otis shuffled over to him and Ribbit guided his stubby hands to what he had found.

"It's a root, Ribbit! Good going! This will definitely catch fire. Now, all we have to do is pull it from the wall."

Easier said than done. Ribbit yanked and tugged at the root, but it simply wouldn't budge. Suddenly, he had a brilliant idea.

"Mr. Turtle, hand me your stone," he said, reaching his hand out. Otis gently placed his rock in Ribbit's palm and Ribbit smashed it against the wall.

"Whoa! I'm excited, too, Ribbit, but let's not get too hasty! Breaking stones will do us no good right now."

"No, Mr. Turtle. I am breaking the rock to make it sharper so I can cut down this root here," Ribbit said, already busily cutting away at the root.

"That'a frog! There you go using that powerful weapon of yours! It's more powerful that you imagined, huh?" Otis said proudly.

"I guess so," Ribbit shrugged as he cut through the layers of the root and heard it fall to the ground with a thud.

*****

203

Phinn looked nervously behind his shoulder, as he bolted down the corridor and came to an abrupt stop. The good news was there was no sight of the lizards behind them, though he could hear their voices echoing in the distance. The bad news was they were at a dead end.

"Where do we go from here?" Croak panted.

Just then, Phinn noticed something. "Hey, does it seem a little brighter to you?"

"Umm . . . yeah. I guess it does," Croak shrugged.

Phinn looked around and was ecstatic to see light streaming in from above them.

"Look!" he cried. "Up there! It's the entrance!" Phinn pointed gleefully.

Phinn noticed that three of the torches were missing from the wall and that settled it. They were back at the entrance.

The echoing voices began to get louder. The lizards were getting closer.

"Quick! Start climbing!" Phinn whispered. The two frogs began scaling the wall, reaching for every nook they could get their fingers into and hoisting themselves toward the light.

Within moments, they scrambled out from underneath the giant boulder and wriggled their way back through the briar patch toward Ollie, toward help. They had made it. They were free!

Rescuing the Rescuer

After what seemed like hours of scraping two rocks together, Otis was finally able to get a spark. Ribbit had never been more excited to see a spark in his whole life! Otis quickly aimed the spark toward a piece of bark that he had stripped off the root and it quickly caught fire. He then carefully brought the smoldering bark over to the rest of the root, which he had stripped into many small pieces. Almost immediately, they had a nice flickering fire.

Ribbit had always had fires at his house. In fact, almost every night his father would light a fire for Ribbit's family to gather around and read stories in front of. Ribbit had never even given starting a fire a second thought. He had always seen his dad use matches and light the wooden logs with ease, but this was nothing like that. This method took patience and effort . . . lots of effort. As he watched Otis's face, lit by the glow of the small fire he had created, Ribbit knew at that moment that he would never look at fire the same way.

"Way to go, Mr. Turtle!" he exclaimed, giving Otis a high five in front of the dancing flames.

"Couldn't have done it without you, Ribbit," Otis replied. "Now, let's get to work."

Ribbit and Otis sat together on the dirt floor and used their fingers to draw out a map and figure out a plan for when they were rescued. They weren't going to be passive anymore.

*****

Phinn spotted Ollie through the thorny briar patch and let out a shriek. Both frogs shot out of the twisted branches, not noticing the scratches they were accumulating this time. They rushed toward Ollie and filled him in on what happened in the cavern. They hardly took a breath, chattering over one another, until the story was told. Phinn told him all about Alexander being Lex, and Croak let him know about almost getting captured and Ribbit being who-knows-where. Phinn was just as surprised at that news as Ollie and gave Croak a hard jab in the ribcage for not telling him the truth.

Ollie's eyes gazed toward the sky, as if he were silently devising a plan. Finally, he spoke.

"Alright, Phinnius and Croak, here's what we need to do. You two are going to have to go back into that cavern."

"You've got to be kidding me!" Phinn cried out, throwing his arms in the air and rolling his eyes.

"What'd you want us to do that for?" Croak said, looking at Ollie as if he had gone mad.

"I need you two to go back down there and lure the lizards out," Ollie said. Croak and Phinn's reluctant reactions were not affecting him at all.

"Oh, no, no, no!" Phinn yelled with his arms crossed and his eyes shut.

"Would you like to hear my plan or would you like to continue ranting and raving, Phinnius?" Ollie said coolly.

Phinn looked at Ollie, then at Croak and plopped down on the ground.

"Fine. Let's hear the plan," he scowled.

"Alright. Here's what we'll do. I will tie two vines around your waist and lower you both down into the cavern at the opening you were telling me about. Then I'm going to need you both to make a ruckus to get their attention. I'm betting that Lex won't be the first one to come out. If he is the ringleader, as you say, then he'll send his two minions out first."

"What the heck are 'minions'?" Croak asked, tilting his head in confusion.

"Let the man finish!" Phinn said exasperatedly, hitting Croak in the arm.

"I'm referring to Canker and Boomer," Ollie said with a wink and a smile. "Anyway, back to the plan. You'll both make a lot of noise to lure Canker and Boomer toward you. When they get within sight, all you have to do is tug on your vine twice and I'll pull you up. I'll perch myself on top of the giant boulder, so I won't be very far. When you give me the signal, I'll keep the vines tightly in my beak and take off into the sky. Then I'll drop the two of you off outside of the briar patch and into safety. Once the lizards are out, I will swoop back around and grab them with my talons and fly them far away."

Ollie noticed both Phinn and Croak glance down at his gnarled left foot. He looked down at the remnant of where his third talon used to be and quickly added, "Now don't underestimate me because of my handicap, my amphibian friends. I may not be the owl I used to be, but I manage just fine."

"We know you will, Ollie," Croak reassured, patting Ollie's feathered back.

Ollie took his gaze off of his foot and straightened up. "Once I have disposed of those wretched lizards, I will come back around, grab you two, and bring you back to the entrance of the cavern. Then you can go back in and rescue Ribbit."

"Okay," Croak smiled.

"It sounds like a good plan, but you are forgetting one thing: Lex! You know, that crazy lizard who is out to kill us all!" Phinn panicked.

"Oh, I haven't forgotten about Lex, Phinnius. However, I'm afraid that you're going to have to battle him on your own. Unless he comes out from beneath the boulder, which I presume he will be smart enough not to once he sees his minions haven't returned, then you are going to have to figure out your own plan of defeating him. I can help you with his two goons, but unfortunately, I cannot help you with him."

Phinn and Croak both let out a giant gulp and exchanged a frightened look.

"Boy, am I going to regret this," Phinn said, standing up straight and putting his hand out in front of him.

Croak placed his hand on top of Phinn's and Ollie placed his wing on the very top.

"Let's get those nasty lizards! 1-2-3 LEAP!" Croak called out as the three friends lifted their hands and began preparing for the battle ahead.

*****

"So once we get him outside, we'll give Ollie the signal to swoop in and grab him" Ribbit said, pointing to the scribbles Otis had made in the dirt. Little did he know how similar his plan was to the very plan his friends had devised moments before.

"Sounds good to me," Otis beamed, his grin illuminated by the fire. "I can't wait to see the look on Lex's face when a giant owl gets him in its grasp!"

"Let's just hope it all works out that way," Ribbit added, looking up into the darkness above.

"Have a little faith, Ribbit. Our plan is better than nothing." Otis patted Ribbit gently on the back. "Besides, sometimes the outcome is better when things don't go as planned."

Ribbit knew he was right. That was almost exactly what Ollie had said to him back at the Enchanted Meadow. He hadn't planned on meeting Ollie or Shelly or Myrtle and look how that turned out. If he hadn't met them, he wouldn't have gotten this far. He was just going to have to try and hope for the best.

*****

Ollie landed on the giant boulder with Phinn and Croak in tow. When he was steady, the two frogs leapt off of his back and made their way toward the entrance of the cavern. Vines were tightly secured around their waists and Ollie held onto the ends with his beak. With a nod, Croak jumped down into the cavern, shortly followed by Phinn. The vines tightened as the two frogs disappeared from sight.

Phinn and Croak hung limply, their toes about a foot from the cold, hard ground. Phinn's stomach twisted. Fear settled on him like a dark fog. He never imagined he would voluntarily come back to this place, not in a million years.

"You ready?" Phinn gulped, the tight vine creating a ripple on his smooth skin.

"Yep," Croak wheezed as he tugged at his vine.

"Here goes nothin'," Phinn said quietly. He sucked in his breath and tried to make a noise, but nothing came out. Fear had constricted his throat and had taken his voice. He cleared his throat and tried again. This time, the thought of the consequences of their plan failing restored his voice. He had to do it for Ribbit.

"AHHH!! WE'RE HERE! HELLO? COME AND GET US! WOO-HOO!" His voice shattered the silence like a hammer on glass, reverberating off the rocky walls throughout the long corridors.

Almost immediately they could hear the scraping of claws against the rocky floor and the swishing sound of movement in the distance. The noises came closer and closer.

They were near.

"PULL US UP! PULL US UP!" Phinn desperately jerked his vine. Although he knew it was impossible for Ollie to hear him, he couldn't help yelling out commands anyway.

Croak also tugged at his vine frantically. He could see the dark outline of two lizards scurrying down the long corridor in their direction, their black eyes gleaming in the torchlight.

"Ooh, I'm gonna get those nasty little frogs for whacking me in the head!" Canker's voice echoed in the distance.

From up top, Ollie felt the vines yank and quickly took off into the air. Before they even had a chance to scream, Phinn and Croak were launched upward out of the cavern and into the sky.

Ollie quickly flew the boys to the open area just outside the briar patch where they had met before. Then, without a word, he took off, back in the direction of the boulder.

Phinn and Croak untangled themselves from their vine supports. By the time they were freed, they could hear some noises coming from the briar patch. It was happening: Ollie was fighting off Canker and Boomer. They could hear it all unfolding. Phinn attempted to peer through the gnarled branches to see what was going on, but all he could see was movement in the distance. He jumped on Croak's shoulder, hoping he could see over the patch. Still, no luck.

It wasn't long before Ollie ascended into the sky, grasping two flailing lizards tightly in his talons. They wriggled and writhed, trying to escape his grips, but Ollie held them securely around their midsections as he flew higher and higher. Phinn and Croak watched as Ollie flew out of sight.

That was their cue. With those two menaces out of their way, it was time for them to head back to the cavern and rescue Ribbit.

*****

"What was that?" Ribbit asked, pausing to listen carefully.

"I don't know. I heard it, too," Otis said, freezing his body and straining his ears.

"It sounds like somebody's coming!" Ribbit whispered anxiously. He wasn't sure if he should be happy or scared. On the one hand, it could be someone coming to rescue him. On the other hand, it could be Lex coming to sentence him to his doom.

"Put out the fire," Otis said, kicking dirt onto the flames.

Once the fire was down to a smoldering ash, the two prisoners stood there waiting; waiting to see a face, waiting to see a friend. Suddenly, a vine tumbled down the side of the hole.

"Whoo-hoo!" Ribbit cried out gleefully. *We've been rescued!*

Otis simply smiled, looked Ribbit square in the eyes, and said, "I told you this isn't how our story ends."

Ribbit chuckled as he grabbed hold of the vine, tugged on it to make sure that it was secure, and then began scaling the side of the hole on his way to freedom. Otis followed closely behind.

Ribbit hoisted himself over the ledge, grasping at the ground around him. He had made it to the top. He expected his buddies to run up and greet him. He expected a warm embrace and a friendly hello. However, looking around, the place was empty. It looked as if he was in another chamber, like the one he had confronted Lex in. The chamber was deserted and silent as if there were no other animals in the world.

"Hello?" Ribbit called out, his voice echoing. "Guys?"

Otis finally wriggled his way to the surface. "Where is everyone?" he asked, inspecting the vine that seemed to be tied around a sturdy stalagmite.

"Well, well well . . ." another voice spoke from the darkness. "So glad you could join me."

"Lex," Ribbit exhaled. His heart sank. This wasn't a rescue.

"What do you want from us, Alexander?" Otis said sternly, looking all around him for any sign of his sneaky foe.

"Leverage. I want leverage," Lex hissed, his voice echoed in every direction.

"What do you mean that you want *leverage*?" Ribbit asked. He didn't know what leverage was, but he was certain that he didn't want to be Lex's leverage.

Lex stepped out from the darkness and into the dimly light chamber. His once friendly face now looked devious and dastardly. Ribbit wasn't sure if it was because he knew what a horrible lizard Lex was or if Lex was showing his true self. Either way, it was ugly.

"It means that you're my ticket out of here."

"What on earth are you talking about?" Otis said as his eyes seared into those of his longtime "friend."

"It seems as though the rescue brigade has arrived and taken off with my accomplices. Therefore, I'm using you two as leverage to ensure that I get outta here alive."

"What does that mean?" Ribbit said, his fists clenched as his frustration bubbled over. It was really beginning to bug him that he had no clue what Lex was blabbering about.

"It means that he is going to hold us hostage and threaten to kill one of us if they try to capture him." Otis glared at Lex with disgust.

"You got that right. If I'm going down, I'm taking one of you with me."

Just then, Ribbit noticed that Lex held a gleaming dagger in his hand. He slithered closer to Otis and Ribbit, his gaze jumping from one to the other.

"Take me. Let the boy go," Otis cried out, stepping in front of Ribbit.

"Oh! Such nobility!" Lex sneered. "That's what I always liked about you, Otis. You'd give up your life for a stranger."

"I guess I had more strangers in my life than I even knew about, Alexander, or should I call you Lex?" Otis snapped.

Lex winced. "Ouch! No need to get feisty now, Otis. It's nothing personal. I really did like you as a friend and I didn't want things to be this way. I really didn't. You're the one who got yourself into this mess. If you would've just delivered those spiders, we wouldn't be in this predicament right now."

"Oh, shut it, Alexander! You fooled me. You fooled us all into thinking that you were a descent guy, when what you *really* are is a fraud. I would never knowingly associate myself with the likes of you." Otis's words cut like a knife.

Lex began breathing harder. Otis must have gotten to him. "Alright. That's enough, Otis. It's time to get back to the job at hand. And to show you that our friendship meant something, I'm taking the frog."

"Oh, no you're not!" Croak's voice bellowed from the doorway to the chamber. He and Phinn blocked the doorway, each holding their torch and wearing an expression that said that they meant business.

"Back for more, little froggies?" Lex stared icily at the intruders.

"We've come for our friend . . . or friends." Croak glanced over at Mr. Turtle with a look of confusion. "And we aren't leaving without them." He stepped toward Lex, his torch held high. Phinn crept in behind him. He tried to look intimidating by holding his torch out in front of him, but the more he tried, the sillier he looked.

Lex scoffed at the frogs who were trying their hardest to put on a front of bravery. "Get real. Who you really came for is Ribbit, not the old Turtle. So if you want him . . ." He slithered over toward Ribbit, clutching him tightly from behind, his dagger held tightly at his throat. "Come and get him."

Ribbit's knees began to tremble. His breathing was coming so hard and so fast that he nearly passed out. His head tingling, his body limp, all he could do was stand there, helplessly watching the scene unfold. *Helpless.* He was really getting tired of being the one who had to be rescued. That was supposed to be his job, his mission. He was the rescuer, not the rescue-ee. This is not how things were supposed to be.

For a moment, Croak and Phinn stood still, contemplating their next move.

"Well?" Lex hissed. "What are you waiting for? Or, are you too afraid, little froggies?"

Croak stared straight ahead—straight at Ribbit whose life was in the hands of a psychopath. What could he do? Lex had Ribbit by the throat and at any given moment he could slide his dagger in deep and take Ribbit's life. He had to do something. There had to be a way to distract him or knock him out . . .

Suddenly, Croak was hit with an idea—a brilliantly obvious idea. He slowly put down his torch and held his hands up in surrender. "You got us, Lex. You got us."

"What are you doing?" Phinn spat out, looking at Croak as if he were crazy.

"He's got us," Croak said, his jaw clenched and his eyes open wide.

Phinn could tell by Croak's unusual behavior that something was up. He just hoped that Croak knew what he was doing.

Trusting in his friend, Phinn laid his torch down beside Croak's now smoldering torch and flung his arms toward the ceiling. "Alright, you got us," he mumbled, his eyes wandering in Croak's direction.

"Well, it's nice to see that you boys finally came to your senses. I didn't want it to come to this, but I guess you have left me no choice. It's a shame that you couldn't just mind your own business. But, NOO! You just had to meddle. And look where that's gotten you? Now, I have to kill you all. I can't have you escaping and blabbing my plans to everyone. I simply can't have that." Grasping tightly to his dagger, Lex gazed down upon Ribbit. "And I'll start with you, Ribbit. Good-bye, little froggy," he said, his voice a ghostly whisper.

A trembling Ribbit stared up at the black, lifeless eyes of his enemy. *The last eyes I will ever see,* he thought to himself. The dagger felt cold against the smooth skin on his neck. His life was about to end. Lex was going to win and all was lost. He had to accept that now. Lex had him right where he wanted him. There was nothing he could do.

Croak quickly reached into his vest pocket and pulled out a stone that he had been saving. It was a purple, rigid, crystal-like stone. He had found it by the river, just before they had been attacked by the snake, and was planning on bringing it home as a souvenir. However, desperate times called for desperate measures.

In the blink of an eye, Croak retrieved the stone from his pocket and launched it directly at Lex's right eye. Fortunately, the

217

stone made impact.

Lex howled in pain. He reached both hands toward his injured eye, freeing Ribbit from his grip. As soon as he felt the dagger drop from his neck, Ribbit rushed toward his friends. The three of them started to leap out of there, when Ribbit suddenly stopped.

Mr. Turtle.

He couldn't leave Otis behind with that crazy lunatic.

"Come on, Mr. Turtle! Let's get out of here," Ribbit waved, gasping for air. Lex was still writhing in pain, but it wouldn't be long before he would return to his senses and come looking for revenge.

"Mr. Turtle?" Croak asked Ribbit, his eyes fixed on the old turtle as he crept his way along the corridor.

"You mean *the* Mr. Turtle? Shelly's father? Myrtle's husband? That Mr. Turtle? You've got to be kidding me!" Phinn cried out, putting both of his hands on top of his head. "What are the odds?"

"Nice to meet you, too. Time to get going now. No time for niceties," Otis remarked as he made his way after the three frogs.

Otis headed after the boys, but he couldn't keep up with their pace. He followed them through the winding corridors but began to fall behind.

"Go on without me," he instructed. "I'll be fine. I've handled Lex before. Besides, I need you to get up there and start getting our plan in action. So, go! Get out of here!" He motioned with his stubby hand.

Ribbit knew that there was no use arguing. Otis was right. They all had a better chance of surviving if they went on without him. As much as it pained him to leave Otis behind, he had to get Ollie ready for action in order to save them all.

Operation Owl

Once they were safely out of the cavern, Ribbit quickly filled Ollie in on the plan that he and Otis had come up with. Nightfall was coming and they had to act fast before sunset. Ribbit was happy to find out that Ollie had gotten rid of Canker and Boomer. That was one less thing to worry about. Now all that was left to do was have Ollie fly Phinn and Croak to safety, while Ribbit stood in front of the entrance, enticing Lex to stand on the X that they had scribbled in the dirt. Once Lex was on the X, Ollie would swoop in and carry him away—far away.

Ribbit waved goodbye to his friends as Ollie took off, leaving him alone in the center of the clearing. Though he knew his wait wouldn't be long, Ribbit hated just standing there. Waiting for Lex to come out of the cavern. Waiting to face his foe. Waiting for action. Every fiber in his being screamed for him to run, but he had to think with his heart, not his head. If this plan was going to work, he was going to have to put himself out there. There was no way around it.

Just then, he saw movement from the entrance of the cave. His heart leapt into his throat. This was it: the final showdown.

Lex slid himself effortlessly out of the opening under the giant boulder. His mangled eye was pink and swollen, blood oozing from the corner. Ribbit had no doubt he would never be able to see from that eye again. He snickered as he remembered Ollie's story and he wondered if it was coincidence or fate that led both villains to lose an eye.

"Foolisssh, foolissssh frog," Lex sniveled. "Didn't run away like your little friends." He panted, his awful dagger shining in what little daylight peeked through the clouds. "No . . . you're the brave one," he went on. "I knew you couldn't just slink away like the others. You came here with a purpossse," he hissed.

"Yeah, I did come here with a purpose—getting our flies back," Ribbit gulped. *Play it cool, be brave Ribbit*, he assured himself before continuing. "But now, Lex, I have a new purpose: destroying you." Ribbit couldn't believe how confident he sounded. The words came out perfectly, like something out of one of his fantasies. Only this was no fantasy. This was more real than any-thing he had ever known.

"Oh, really," Lex seethed. "You actually think you can destroy me. Ha!" He tilted his head back for dramatic effect. "Well then, little frog, come and get me." Still clutching his dagger, he stepped closer to Ribbit, closer to the X, but not quite on the mark.

Ribbit desperately looked toward the sky. Where was Ollie? He couldn't stall Lex any longer. He knew that Lex was ready to pounce at any given moment. His only hope was to get him on the X and pray that Ollie would swoop in. But he wasn't on the X yet. He still had another foot to go. Ribbit had to think fast. He was going to have to get Lex to come to him.

"It's always me who has to come to you. Are you too much of a coward to come and get me, Lex?" Ribbit taunted. His pulse quickened and his palms were sweating. He had to play it cool.

Lex laughed scornfully. "I just figured you might want to take what last little power you have left to get in the first shot. But, have it your way!" Lex lurched toward Ribbit, his feet crossing over the X.

For a terrible moment, Ribbit thought that Lex was going to tear him to pieces. He wished that he could disappear—just dissolve into thin air. His mind was a blur with all of the events that had led him here. Events that had led him to this very moment where he had laughed in the face of danger and put himself smack-dab in the middle of harm's way. He wished that he could see his family one last time. Wished that he could hug his mom and dad and Zippy. Wished he could enjoy a delicious mosquito milkshake or his mother's fly stew one last time. Wished that he could be back home.

Ribbit winced, bracing for impact, but instead, Lex's wail filled the air. His voice was as shrill as nails on a chalkboard. *Was it a war cry or a cry for help?* Ribbit opened his eyes to find out. He was surprised to see nothing in front of him. No Lex. No dagger.

Lex dangled high in the air, stabbing his dagger into the nothingness that surrounded him and wriggling around like a fish out of water. Ollie's sharp talons held tightly onto Lex's tail, keeping his dagger as far away from him as he could. Ollie had never looked so majestic; his giant brown spotted wings beating furiously.

"Whoo-hoo! You did it, Ollie! Way to go!" Ribbit cried out gleefully. He jumped in the air victoriously, punching his arms toward the sky, as the giant bird flapped overhead.

"AHHHH! LET GO OF ME, EVIL BIRD!" Lex yelled.

"Not a chance," Ollie said coolly. "I'm going to take you somewhere where you won't be able to hurt anyone ever again." With that, Ollie flew higher into the sky, his flailing prey dangling from his grips.

Ribbit hurried through the briar patch to meet up with his friends. He felt such a rush of adrenaline that he didn't even notice the many thorns scraping at his limbs, though he knew that he probably had more scratches on him than he had skin intact. He didn't care. He was free! They all were free!

*****

Ollie held on tightly to Lex's scaly tail. He knew exactly where he was going. There was a small island not far from where the river met the ocean. He had already dropped Canker and Boomer off there, so he knew the route fairly well. He had to make haste, as the sun was quickly setting and darkness would be upon them soon.

"Let me go, you flying demon!" Lex cried out, still wriggling furiously.

"Oh, I will. When we get there."

"Get where? Are you going to eat me?" Lex whimpered.

"Believe me, if that were my intention, I would've eaten you already."

"Then what are you going to do with me?"

"As I said before, I'm going to put you some place where you will never be able to hurt anyone ever again," Ollie said sternly, looking toward the vast ocean in the distance. They were getting closer.

"Not if I have anything to do with it," Lex mumbled.

"What was that?" Ollie strained to hear Lex's words.

Silence.

"Decided to give up, Lex?" Ollie chuckled, looking down in Lex's direction.

Ollie let out a gasp. Lex was gone.

And in his talons, Ollie still held tightly to Lex's tail, which was no longer attached to his reptilian body.

Lex had escaped.

The Long Journey Home

The three frogs greeted Ollie with a cheer of victory as he descended from the navy blue sky. His giant wings created a gust of wind that caressed Ribbit's face as if sweeping his worries away. The large owl warmly embraced his friends and smiled at their cheerfulness. On the exterior he seemed fine; however, his eyes told a different story. He was holding something back.

"Is everything alright, Ollie?" Ribbit asked. Phinn and Croak ignored his question and continued celebrating, skipping around with glee.

"Well . . ." Ollie looked down at something clenched tightly in his talons. "Unfortunately, there was a setback in the plan."

"What do you mean there was a setback?" Phinn asked, the joy instantly draining from his face. His skipping ceased; Croak's celebrating also screeched to a halt.

"What's going on, Ollie? Is it Lex? What happened?" Ribbit's mind was a flurry.

"I had to hold Lex by his tail in order to keep his dagger away and in all of the excitement it slipped my mind that lizards have the ability to shed their tails in the face of danger." Ollie lifted up his foot and released Lex's tail from his talons. It fell limp on the ground. "I'm afraid Lex got away." Ollie trailed off, tears welling in his round, yellow eyes.

"Hey, don't be hard on yourself, Ollie. You couldn't have predicted this would happen." Ribbit patted the owl on his back. "And the important thing is that we're all safe and those evil lizards are far, far away." It broke Ribbit's heart to see Ollie so upset. After all, Ollie was a hero. He had saved his life—their lives—several times now. The last thing that he should be feeling is disappointed in himself.

Croak stepped over to the large owl and put his arm around Ollie. "Yeah, you did good, big guy. You did good."

"But I failed you. I'm so sorry," Ollie mumbled, still looking at the ground.

Phinn hopped under Ollie's head, directly under his gaze. He looked the old owl straight in the eye and said, "Ollie, if it weren't for you, I wouldn't be here. None of us would be here. And that, dear owl, makes you a hero. Besides, Lex probably didn't survive the drop. You were flying pretty high up."

"How did you get to be the sensible one in all of this,

Phinnius?" Ollie chuckled. "And how did I end up the blubber-head?"

They all shared in a good laugh.

We did it! Ribbit thought to himself. Then he glanced over at his buddies. Their skin was riddled with pink scratches, their once neat clothes now in tatters. There was no way he could have done any of this, had any of these adventures, without the help of his friends. And now he would be returning home with new friends: Ollie, Ophelia, Shelly, Myrtle . . . *Oh, no!* Ribbit shot up.

"Mr. Turtle! How could we forget?" He gasped. He turned and quickly headed toward the briar patch. "We have to go back for him!"

Without uttering a word, Phinn and Croak headed after Ribbit, while Ollie took off toward the giant boulder.

"Mr. Turtle! We're coming! We're coming! Stay put!" Ribbit yelled out, making his way through the thorns. He hoped that he would never have to see another briar patch after this again! His torn up skin agreed with him.

He could see the clearing ahead and cried out again. "Mr. Turtle! We're on our way! We're com—" Ribbit stopped mid-sentence as he entered the clearing and found Otis standing outside the boulder, completely unharmed.

"Mr. Turtle!" Ribbit panted. "Are you okay? Is everything alright?"

"Relax, relax. I'm fine. I guess Lex's eye injury was pretty severe. Ran right past me. Probably thought I was a rock in that dim lighting. Good throw by the way," Otis winked at Croak. "Did it work? Our plan?"

"Sorta," Ribbit shrugged. "Ollie flew him pretty far away, but Lex escaped."

"Oh, well. Just as long as everyone's safe, that's all that really matters. We can always deal with Lex another day." Otis smiled. His eyes made their way to Ollie. "Wow! This must be your owl friend. I'm Otis." He bowed at the enormous bird.

"Pleasure to meet you, Otis. My name is Ollie." Ollie bowed back.

"Oh, before I forget, I picked this up when I was down there. Nearly tripped over the thing on my way out." Otis reached behind his back and pulled out Ribbit's pack.

"My pack! Thank you! Thank you! Thank you!" Ribbit cried. It felt so good to see it again. Just holding it made him feel better. Besides, he knew that he would never be able to replace his R.T. Hopkins book or the book Shelly gave him. At that moment he vowed to never let them out of his sights again.

Overwhelmed with joy, Ribbit squeezed Mr. Turtle in a big hug around his neck. He couldn't wait to get Mr. Turtle home to Shelly and Myrtle, where he belonged. He knew that they would be ecstatic to see him.

"Alright, everyone. Let's get out of this treacherous place and go home," Ollie sang out. "First things first." He hopped over to the large pods containing the thousands of flies and mosquitoes that had been missing. With his sharp beak, he pecked the pods open, one at a time, letting all of the insects swarm out like a huge, delicious tidal wave.

"Wait!" Ribbit cried out before Ollie pecked open the last pod. "Do you think that we could save that one and bring it back to Lily Pad Hollow? We're a long way from home and I know that all of the frogs there could really use some flies about now."

"Plus, we need evidence that this whole thing really happened," Phinn chimed in, pointing toward the sky.

"Of course we can," Ollie said. "Why don't you all hop on my back so I can take you home. I'll grab hold of the pod with my talons and you can take it back to Lily Pad Hollow with you."

Ribbit's heart leapt at the sound of the word *home*. He wasn't just going back to Lily Pad Hollow. He was going back home. Home to his parents. Home to Zippy. Home to the pond. *Home.*

"All aboard! Next stop, the Turtle home," Ollie sang out cheerfully.

They all jumped onto Ollie's back and held tight as the giant bird took flight into the night sky, the stars twinkling in celebration of their great achievement.

After a while, Ollie began to descend from the sky. Down below, they could see the grassy knoll of the Turtle home. Smoke drifted lazily from the stone fireplace and a warm glow radiated from the windows. Beside the knoll, the river drifted lazily, the stars mirrored in its glassy surface. Ribbit glanced over at Otis, who gently wiped a tear from his eye. He was glad that he could be a part of reuniting him with Shelly and Myrtle. He felt as if, in some small way, he was returning the favor for the Turtles saving his life.

Ollie swooped down, gently landing on the spongy grass just outside the Turtle home. Otis dismounted then turned to face his friends.

"Thank you. Thank you, for everything," he said sincerely, bowing his head to show his gratitude.

Ollie bowed back at the old turtle.

"Anything for a friend," Ribbit waved. Phinn nodded his head in agreement.

"See ya, Mr. T!" Croak bellowed from atop the great owl's back.

"Good-bye, my friends. You truly are heroes to me." And with that, Otis turned around, opened the door, and stepped into his house. Almost instantly, they could hear the joyful cheers of a family reuniting as Ollie batted his giant wings and they took off into the night sky once again. The three frogs peered down and could faintly see the Turtle family exit their house and wave at them, calling out words of appreciation. The frogs waved back. Ribbit cupped his hands over his mouth and yelled out, "Just returning the favor! Hope to see you soon!" And they were off.

"Is it all right if I make one quick stop before I take you boys home?" Ollie said. "I must check in on Momma and my little ones so they don't worry."

"Of course, Ollie," Ribbit said as he gripped tightly onto the feathers on his back. The others echoed his sentiment.

"Yeah, and I need some grub!" Croak rubbed his round belly.

It suddenly occurred to Ribbit that they hadn't eaten since breakfast, except for the few runaway flies they caught outside the pods. He had been running on so much adrenaline that he hadn't even noticed the rumbling in his stomach.

"I think we could all use a little nourishment," Ollie added.

"I'm so hungry you're actually starting to look pretty delicious, Phinn," Croak wailed, as they all burst out in laughter. It was the first time since he had sat by the pond's edge sipping mosquito milkshakes that Ribbit had felt carefree enough to share in a good laugh without any hesitations. Their mission was complete and he could get back to just being a young frog again—to just being Ribbit McFly.

*****

Back at the great oak tree, Ribbit gobbled up Momma's cooking with such intensity that he almost choked more than once. He couldn't help himself.

The large dining room was filled with the sounds of silverware clanking, mouths smacking, and the grunting of satisfaction with their meal. The children watched in awe as the three frogs stuffed their faces with beetle raviolis, spicy ant tacos, and mashed sow bugs, washing it down with mulled cider. Ribbit could hear them giggling as he shoveled the food into his mouth, but he didn't mind.

When dinner was over, Momma excused the children to get ready for bed. Then she smoothed out the apron that hung tightly around her feathery waist. "So, quite the adventure, huh dearies?"

"That's an understatement," Phinn rolled his eyes playfully. They all laughed.

"Now, it has been a very long day and as much as I know that ya'll are dying to get back home, I insist that you get some rest. It's not safe to be flying under such exhaustion," Momma said, as she began clearing some of the empty serving dishes off of the table.

"Aw, pondscum," Ribbit mumbled. He was anxious to get home. He didn't care about sleeping. Who could sleep at a time like this? All he wanted to do was get back to his family. Phinn and Croak's whines implied that they felt the same way.

"I'm afraid Momma is right. We need to reenergize before our big departure. Lily Pad Hollow will still be there in the morning," Ollie said kindly, as if he could read Ribbit's thoughts. "Plus, it will be better for you to have your energy for all of the greetings and warm welcomes you'll receive. Remember, you aren't just returning home the same frogs that you used to be. You are returning home as heroes." He gave a little wink, before placing his napkin on the table, picking up his plate, and walking toward the kitchen where Momma was washing off the dishes and cooing a gentle tune.

As much as Ribbit hated to admit it, they were right. The three frogs helped clear the table, then tiptoed back up to the library, and turned in for their last night of rest before returning home.

A Triumphant Return

It was still dark outside when Ribbit heard a knock on the library door. He shot up instantly, as did Phinn and Croak. Although they had been resting, their excitement for the day ahead left them in a very light sleep. It reminded Ribbit of the sleep he got the night before they left Lily Pad Hollow.

Ollie quietly slipped into the room and greeted the boys with a gentle smile. "Alright, my little amphibian friends. Are you ready to get going?" he whispered.

"You betchya!" Ribbit exclaimed cheerfully, swinging his legs out of the covers.

"Am I ready? I've been ready since the day we left!" Phinn yawned.

Croak sat up, rubbing his eyes. He wasn't much of a morning frog, so they probably wouldn't hear much from him until they got home.

The boys swiftly gathered their belongings and followed Ollie downstairs. Outside, the crickets still sang their nighttime melody, but were accompanied by the twitter of small birds summoning the morning to come.

Momma whipped up a quick snack of sugared moths for them to take on their travels. She made them promise that they would come back and visit again. They assured her they would as they gave her a big hug (except Ollie who gently kissed her on the cheek). Then they walked outside into the cool morning air.

Ollie looked around. The sun hadn't risen yet and the stars still lightly blinked cheerfully in the sky. "I've never been to Lily Pad Hollow before, so I'm going to need some guidance. How about an estimate of the direction that you came from? Was it north, south, east, or west?" Ollie pointed his giant wing.

"Uh . . . uh . . ." Ribbit hesitated. He wasn't sure what direction they had come from. It all seemed like a blur to him. It felt like it was a million years ago that they left Lily Pad Hollow and began their adventure.

"If my memory serves me, we came due east," Phinn chimed in, a smug look on his face.

"Does that sound right to you, Ribbit? Croak?" Ollie asked.

"Uh . . . sure," Ribbit shrugged.

"Don't look at me. Whatever he said," Croak tilted his head in Phinn's direction.

"East it is. Lily Pad Hollow, here we come!" Ollie spread out his enormous wings, grasped the precious fly pod tightly with his talons, and took flight.

Ribbit took one last look at the Enchanted Meadow. It's magic and beauty shone through the darkness. Ribbit knew it wouldn't be the last time he saw the meadow—it just couldn't be. He'd return one day, that much he was sure of. He silently whispered words of good-bye to the place that had changed his life forever, and then turned to face home.

*****

As the sun peeked over the horizon with the promise of a beautiful day, Ribbit peered down over Ollie's wing and spotted a familiar sight: a dense gathering of reeds.

"Hey, guys! We're getting close! I think I can see the Great Reed Barrier down below!" Ribbit cried out. He was so excited he could feel his heart pounding in his ears.

"You're right! I can see the cattails up ahead!" Phinn sang out, pointing down at the cattails. Their dancing in the slight morning breeze no longer held the same spell over Ribbit as it had nearly a week ago. He had crossed their borders—seen the unseen. Now all he wanted to do was go home.

"Whoo-hoo!" Croak screamed, his hands clenched in fists and held high in the air.

"Hey, Ollie! I think you better bring us down here!" Ribbit called out to the giant owl.

"Alright. Down we go. Prepare for descent!" Ollie swiftly swooped down and landed carefully in the thick gathering of cattails, bending many of their stems in an effort to land on solid ground.

"This isn't quite what I expected your Lily Pad Hollow to look like," Ollie remarked, handing the fly pod over to Croak, who beamed at being chosen to be the one to carry it home.

"No, no, no. This isn't home. The Hollow is just through those cattails over there," Ribbit pointed.

"Then why didn't we have him drop us off at home instead of in this shrubbery?" Phinn said, a bit of disturbance shaking in his voice.

"Because we can't very well have an owl flying over Lily Pad Hollow. The Border Patrol would have launched an attack thinking he was an enemy or something," Ribbit said, feeling proud that he had been clearheaded enough to think about those consequences ahead of time. He definitely was a different frog.

"Good thinking, Ribbit! I could really do without any more attacks coming my way," Ollie winked. "Will you be able to find your way home from here?"

"Yeah, I think so," Ribbit nodded.

"Alright then, my little amphibian friends, I guess this is good-bye." They all gave Ollie a great big hug, squeezing the life out of him.

"Thank you, Ollie, for everything," Ribbit whispered still holding tight to Ollie's feathery body.

"It truly was my pleasure. And thank you, for giving me such an adventure," Ollie's voice cracked. "Don't forget about this old bird and do come visit us again soon."

"We could never forget you, Ollie," Ribbit smiled.

After embracing for a moment, the three frogs released Ollie from their grips and stepped back to face their friend, one last time, before Ollie ruffled up his feathers and took off into the sky.

They watched him fly until he was just a dot on the horizon. It was sad to watch him leave. Ribbit was really going to miss him.

"Last one there's a rotten toadstool!" Phinn sprinted into the cattails, their stems wobbling and making a whooshing sound. Ribbit and Croak—with the fly pod in tote— followed quickly behind.

With hearts thumping and spirits high, they scrambled through the dense cattail borders and emerged giddy and triumphant. There it was: home.

Ribbit wondered how he could ever want to leave this place. Lily Pad Hollow was more beautiful than he had remembered. It was dawn and the sleepy town was hushed. The pond's surface sparkled like diamonds winking at the early morning sun. How much had changed since they had been away! The warm, summer days were gone and autumn, Ribbit's favorite time of year, was starting to show. The gentle breeze of daybreak stirred, sending small showers of red, orange, and gold leaves twisting and cascading to the ground.

As families awakened, amber lights lit up the windows of the frog homes, nestled in roots of trees and logs that dotted the pond's edge. Stone fireplaces released puffs of gray smoke, curling and twisting in the crisp autumn air.

"We made it, guys. We're home," Ribbit sighed as he wiped the tears from his eyes. He looked warmly at his buddies. They had been through so much together. Heck, they both nearly died on more than one occasion, and yet they never lost their faith in Ribbit and never, not for one single moment, doubted that he could accomplish what he set out to do. They had been with him on the greatest adventure of his life and for that he would be forever grateful.

"It's about time!" Phinn joked, gently elbowing Ribbit in the ribs. They all laughed, wiping their eyes, their arms slung around each other.

"Think anyone's gonna believe us?" Croak said, looking around the sleepy town.

"They better! I didn't almost get eaten by a snake, fall off a cliff, and fight evil lizards for nothing!" Phinn grinned.

"I think our fly pod here will do all the talking and put a stop to any doubts. Besides, we know the truth of what happened out there and that's all that really matters, guys." Ribbit was surprised that he actually meant it. He didn't care if Squiggy or Kilroy or anyone else believed the great adventure they had been on. They knew what they had experienced and it was a memory they would never forget.

"So, what are we waiting for? Let's go home!" Phinn said anxiously.

The three frogs looked at each other then took off in a full sprint toward home. As they scrambled through the muddy water past the cattail border's edge, they could hear the familiar sounds of home. The Border Patrol caught sight of them instantly and waved their arms, calling out words of greeting from their posts.

Ribbit paid no mind to them. He was on a mission to get home. The frogs raced through the small town, which was beginning to stir with morning activity. Outside the Backwater Café, Mr. Boggy was busy sweeping away the autumn leaves so as not to leave a single one on his front stoop. He looked up from his chore, his face lit with surprise.

"Ribbit, Phinneus, Croak! Good to have you back! We thought you were goners for sure!" He called out. "Can I tempt you with some candied water striders to celebrate your return?"

"No thanks, Mr. Boggy," Ribbit panted as he continued to leap through town. It felt so good to see a familiar face, but he knew how much better it would feel to see his family, and he just couldn't wait any longer to share the good news with them.

Just then, Mr. Boggy's eyes wandered to Croak and his giant cargo. "My word! Are those what I think they are?" He pointed a trembling finger at the fly pod.

"Sure are! And there'll be enough for everyone!" Ribbit cried out cheerfully as he darted away with Phinn and Croak at his side.

Phinn's house was the closest, so naturally, they arrived there first.

"Well, it's been quite the trip," Phinn said, as they opened the squeaky gate made out of sticks that fenced in his yard. He looked up at his friends as if he would never see them again, as if this were the end of their time together.

"Phinn, I can't begin to thank you enough for coming with me and for saving my life. And that goes for you, too, Croak." Ribbit patted his buddies on the back.

"Aw, don't go getting all sappy on us now," Croak joked.

"Yeah, if it were up to me I wouldn't have gone out on that crazy mission! Do you realize that because of your outlandish ideas, we were all almost killed? It's because of you that we were stranded in the wilderness, attacked by a giant snake, got chased through dark, scary caverns . . ." Phinn ranted, his eyes fixed on Ribbit and his arms flailing alternately with each event he listed.

Ribbit sucked in his breath. *Now that it was all over and they were safe at home, was Phinn really upset?* he wondered. *After all, it was my idea and I put them in real danger. I hadn't even thought about that until now. It really was all my fault.*

Ribbit's head drooped down in shame.

"Then again . . ." Phinn added, bending down to meet Ribbit's gaze and bringing his eyes back up. "If you hadn't of forced me to go on this crazy mission, I wouldn't have met Ollie or Shelly or Myrtle or Momma . . . and I wouldn't have had the best time of my life."

Ribbit let out his breath. "You had me going there, you cockroach! I really thought you were upset with me!" Ribbit pointed his finger at his friend, unable to contain his expanding grin. "You know, I should have let those lizards get you. It would serve you right for being such a thorn in my side," he teased. It felt nice for the three of them to laugh again and be carefree like they used to be.

"Well, I guess I should go in," Phinn sighed after the laughing subsided.

"So long, old buddy." Croak put his free hand to his forehead and saluted Phinn.

"Yeah, Phinn. It's been a real adventure," Ribbit added.

Phinn nodded at his companions then turned and walked in the door to his house, letting it swing shut behind him.

And then there were two.

Ribbit and Croak went to Ribbit's house next. Croak's house was closer to Phinn's than Ribbit's was, but they had decided that since it really was Ribbit's mission that he should be the one to return home with the fly pod. And seeing as he was nowhere near strong enough to lug that thing all the way home, Croak offered to drop it off at the McFly house before going home himself.

Ribbit burst into hyper speed as soon as he saw the familiar glow in the windows of the log he called home. They were awake! They were waiting for him! He couldn't wait a second longer to see them, hug them, and tell them about his adventures.

"Mom, Dad, Zippy!" Ribbit cried, making his way up the yard, Croak trailing behind. He wouldn't be able to keep up with

Ribbit's sudden acceleration even if he wasn't carrying a cumbersome sack full of fluttering insects.

"Ribbykins?" Ribbit's mother's voice rang out from inside, accompanied by the crashing sound of dishes being dropped. Her voice sounded uncertain, as if she weren't sure it was really Ribbit or if she were hearing things. "Ribbykins, is that you?"

The front door swung open and there stood Ribbit's mother, her apron disheveled, and her face heavy with worry. She looked older, like this week had worn her down.

"Oh, thank heavens! It is my little Ribbykins!" she sang out. With her head up and her arms held high in the sky, she ran toward Ribbit, and swallowed him up in a warm embrace. Then she covered his face in kisses, holding him snugly to her chest.

"Don't you ever leave like that again!" She said sternly, still holding Ribbit closely to her heart, as if he would disappear if she let go. He could feel her heart thumping with excitement.

"Springer, Zippy, get out here! Our little Ribbykins is home!" She screamed toward the house. Her voice was so loud and shrill that Ribbit could hear ringing in his ears.

Ribbit's dad quickly came into the doorway then ran to greet Ribbit and join his mother in a world-class hug.

"We were so worried about you, kiddo. You don't know what we've been through trying to find you! We had the Border Patrol on double duty . . ." He paused his ranting and looked at his son. Ribbit could see his eyes soften, as if just looking at Ribbit brushed off his worries. "Well, it doesn't matter. All that's important is you are home safe. Welcome home, kiddo."

Just then, Zippy stepped into the doorway, still in her nightshirt, her eyes droopy with sleep. As soon as she saw Ribbit, she shied away, her fingers interlaced, her eyes filled with hurt.

"Hi, Zippy," Ribbit beckoned to his sister, but she hesitated and remained motionless in the doorway. His leaving must have affected her more than he knew.

"Zippy, don't you want to say hello to your brother?" Ribbit's mother implored, pointing at Ribbit with a giant grin on her face.

"No," Zippy insisted sharply, crossing her arms.

"Why not, sweetheart?" Ribbit's father joined in.

"He left me," she began to whimper.

Ribbit untangled himself from his parents' embrace and walked over to Zippy. He squatted down to her level and placed his thumb under her chin. "Hey, I'm sorry I left you. I would never hurt you on purpose, Zippy Lou. I just had a very important job to do. Do you forgive me?"

"No."

"Please, Zippy? I'll play whatever you want to play later, okay? Even Pollies."

Begrudgingly, she smiled. "Okay, Ribbit." She gave him a tight squeeze. "Just don't do it again!"

Ribbit giggled. "I won't have to, Zippy. I found what I was looking for."

"What do you mean you found what you were looking for?" Ribbit's mother asked suspiciously. In all of the excitement, no one had noticed Croak standing there with a giant pod full of flies.

"Take a look for yourself." Ribbit pointed at the pod that Croak had set in their front yard. They all immediately burst out into cheers of joy and celebration as they inspected the pod and greeted Croak.

"How on earth?" his mother gasped.

"Trust me, mom. You wouldn't believe me if I told you," Ribbit laughed.

"Well, I'm gonna need a lot more information than that. But first, let's alert the town. I think a celebration is in order!" Ribbit's father exclaimed as he headed into the house to get dressed.

"This is just the most marvelous day! First my Ribbykins comes home then all of the flies are returned. Oh, happy day!" Ribbit's mother cried out, giving Ribbit another wet kiss on his cheek before she too headed into the house to cook up a hearty breakfast for her son and get ready for the day.

Ribbit picked up Zippy and held her on his hip as he walked over to his friend.

"Thanks for everything, Croak."

"No, prob. I'll see you around, Ribbit." And with that, Croak hopped off toward his small wooden cottage and his family who would be delighted upon his return.

Ribbit felt a pang of sadness watching his buddy hop away. He had been through so much with Croak and Phinn that it felt weird, almost unnatural, for them to part. However, he knew that he would see them again soon. The important thing was that they were home. Finally, they were home.

Something's Missing

Once inside, Ribbit's family huddled in the living room waiting to hear all the details of his grand adventure. So much had happened that he didn't even know where to start! It was as if he couldn't speak fast enough! His excitement took over, causing him to forget important details and mix up the order of things. He constantly interrupted himself with events he had forgotten and he was sure that his story was a jumble. However, his parents and Zippy didn't seem to notice. They were so entranced in his every detail that it didn't matter if some of the events were out of order or that parts of his story simply didn't make sense. They were just delighted to have their son back and to hear about the world outside Lily Pad Hollow.

After his story was told, his parents squeezed him as if there were no tomorrow and told him how proud of him they both were.

Zippy was already busy playing out her own imaginary version of what had happened, pretending as if the couch was Ollie's back and she was soaring high above the world. "Alright, my little tadpoles. I have to tell everyone I know and let them in on the good news. And we must start planning your celebration!" Ribbit's mother sang out cheerfully.

"This party is going to be the biggest one the town has ever seen and it's all for my brave little boy and his two best friends." His father looked proudly at Ribbit, then turned back to Ribbit's mother. "I'll head downtown and get the preparations started! Woohoo!" Ribbit's father exclaimed, putting on his hat and heading out the door. Ribbit hadn't seen him this excited since some of the frogs put on a circus act a year ago.

Ribbit's mother got straight to work telling the neighbors of her son's return, giving Ribbit a moment to unwind and unpack. He hopped into his room and opened the door. How different, and yet the same, it all looked. Everything was where he had left it: his books stacked neatly on his shelf, his drawings sprawled out on his desk, his bed sheets all crumpled from the last night he had slept in them, the night of the great escape. Yet, it all seemed so different because he was different.

He put down his pack and leapt onto his spongy bed, letting his body melt slowly into the soft sheets. It felt like an eternity since he had last slept in it.

He lay there for a while, looking up at the ceiling in silence, going over every detail from his trip. He savored each event and put all the details in order. He knew he would have to share his story with his friends, his classmates, the entire town for that matter, and he would have to do a better job than the chaotic summary he just gave his parents.

After a while, he decided it was time to unpack his belongings and settle back in to being home again. He zipped open his pack and took out his firefly nightlight. The firefly lay sleeping at the bottom of the jar, blissfully unaware of the adventure he had just been on. If only he knew where he had been! Next, Ribbit pulled out *Salamander Sam* and caressed the book lovingly. This book had been the only piece of home Ribbit had taken with him and it had given him great comfort in his time of need. It now felt as if it were a part of him, somehow. He carefully put the book on his bookshelf, facing its cover forward, rather than its spine. This book deserved to be showcased, not stacked with the other books.

Ribbit returned to his pack for one last thing: *Sparrow's Journey Home*. It was now just as precious to him as his beloved *Salamander Sam*.

He reached his hand in and despair washed over him like a wave on the shore. The book was gone. Ribbit frantically turned his pack upside down, hoping it would magically appear, as if it had been trapped in some small compartment somewhere. No such thing happened. His bag was empty.

Bewildered, Ribbit racked his mind for when he last saw the book. Was it in Shelly's fort? Was it in the woods? Did he have it when he was at Ollie's? Was it somewhere in the cavern? He simply couldn't remember. All he knew for sure was that he didn't have it anymore.

Ribbit felt a gripping pain in his heart as he slumped on the floor. His book was gone and there was no replacing it. Misery threatened to overcast an otherwise spectacular day, until the distant sounds of the town preparing for the big celebration, along with the gleeful sound of his mother chatting excitedly with her friends, and Zippy playing her imaginary conquest out in the living room, swept all his sadness away. What was he going on about? He was home! He had gone on an incredible journey, saved the town he loved, and returned safely, and now he was going to be upset over a book? *Forget the book*, he thought. *I have everything I need right here.*

He let out a deep sigh, letting the book go with it. Then, he picked himself up from the floor and changed his clothes into something more presentable. After all, he had a celebration to attend.

A Heroic Celebration

There was an air of excitement buzzing through the tiny hollow. By now almost everyone had heard that Ribbit, Croak, and Phinn had not only come home, but had brought back their beloved flies. Word traveled fast and everyone was already hard at work to create a Welcome Home Harvest Festival in honor of the new town heroes.

The autumn morning glistened, and Lily Pad Hollow was aflutter in anticipation. Mr. Boing, in his signature white apron, swept in front of his hardware shop as his wife busily polished the antique brass lampposts. Hands on her hips, she proudly boasted, "I can see my reflection, plain as day." At the edge of the pond, the Green family was working as a team stringing tiny white lights in the trees. Mayor Cornelius walked around, inspecting all of the carnival stands, and giving thumbs up to all of the frogs who were hard at work setting up the festival. Huge banners were displayed with words of encouragement, such as "Way to go, brave heroes!" "Thank you, thank you, Ribbit, Croak, and Phinn!" and "You did it!!" Along with these, a small yellow banner was being hung across town square reading, "My Brother, My Hero!" Ribbit wondered how Zippy and the Dandelion Girls had found the time to create this poster when he'd only been home for a matter of hours.

Mr. BugEye and his son, Pickles, had raked the autumn leaves that were scattered along Main Street into a large pile near the gooseberry patch. Many of the young frogs leapt merrily into the colorful pile, throwing the leaves into the air like confetti.

Tables with colorful tablecloths were set up in a little meadow behind Mr. Boggy's café. A quaint gazebo was being erected for the band by many of Ribbit's schoolmates who, until this very moment, never thought twice about the odd little frog and his two unusual sidekicks. Mrs. Leapingsworth was handing out snacks of fly chips to all the workers while Zippy and the other Dandelion Girls were busy passing out cups of refreshing fly punch. There was chatter, laughter, and sing-alongs as the residents of Lily Pad Hollow joined together in camaraderie to acknowledge Ribbit, Croak, and Phinn for their courageous feat.

All of Lily Pad Hollow came out to celebrate their return. Frogs large and small lined Main Street, spirits high and faces aglow. Even Old Frog Amphibilus left his porch, which was surprising to Ribbit since he was convinced he was glued to that old rocking chair. The sidewalks were lined with many painted wooden carts in shades of bubble gum, violet, sky blue, and lime, each offering a different fly-flavored treat, such as fly cotton candy, gummy flies, fly fries, fly sausages on a stick, candied flies, and snow cones with a sweet fly syrup on top.

The middle of the street was crowded with cheerful frogs playing carnival games like Pin the Tongue on the Froggy, Bobbing for Water Striders (no tongues allowed), Three-Legged Hop Races, Throw the Stone in the Fishbowl (which Croak was so good at he was asked not to play anymore since there would be no prizes left for the other frogs), a Fly Cake Walk, and Snail Races, where frogs were yelling out words of encouragement for their snail to win. Small frogs gleefully clung to their prizes of stuffed animal snails, firefly-tip wands (that glowed magically adding sparks of colored light throughout the carnival), water guns, and beautiful painted shell maracas.

It was the best party ever and Ribbit was having a blast!

In the middle of an invigorating game of bobbing for water striders, the festivities were suddenly interrupted by the wailing of the Border Patrol warning horns, a sound that was as unfamiliar to the town as the trumpet of an elephant may have been.

The very sound of the alarm sent a ripple through the crowded streets; each frog froze, their conversations ceasing, as if their ears were betraying them, until pandemonium struck. Shrieks of fear accompanied the constant wailing of the warning horns as frogs leapt crazily through the street, disregarding all emergency drill procedures they had practiced every spring. As children scrambled to meet up with their parents and young frogs pushed their way through the crowds, a giant shadow blocked out the sun—a giant shadow in the shape of a bird.

"It's the end of the world! It's the end of the world! I knew I shouldn't have left my porch!" Old Mr. Amphibilus cried out, a horrified expression distorting his face as he pointed in the sky at the giant bird gracefully gliding overhead.

The first person that came into Ribbit's mind was Zippy. He had to find her and make sure that she was safe from danger. Staying surprisingly alert, Ribbit pushed his way through the crowds, desperately searching for a small speckled head among the sea of green.

He cupped his hands over his mouth and called out, "Zippy! Zippy!"

"Ribbit?" a small voice answered. Zippy sat calmly on the curb, as if nothing unusual was going on around her, eating her fly cotton candy which had somehow managed to get stuck all over her face.

"Zippy! Come with me! Where are Mom and Dad?" Ribbit looked around and they were nowhere to be found. Zippy simply shrugged and continued to yank off wads of puffy cotton candy and jam them playfully into her mouth. Ribbit picked his sister up and held her on his hip as she licked her sticky fingers, still completely unaware of the chaos that surrounded her.

Without warning, the giant bird plummeted from the sky.

The crowd of green frogs leapt frantically out of its path. All except for Ribbit.

"How come everyone's going that way?" Zippy asked, pointing to the crowd of screaming frogs dashing into hiding.

Ribbit looked over his left shoulder, then over his right. The once teeming street was empty. They were alone. Ribbit could feel all the frightened eyes staring through the windows of the shops on Main Street. He and Zippy stood in the street as if serving themselves up on a platter.

Before Ribbit could look up, the giant bird landed abruptly in front of him, its wings propelling a whoosh of wind that slapped him so hard in the face that he lost his balance and fell backward onto the unforgiving dirt road. Fortunately, Ribbit's stomach broke Zippy's fall and she was completely unharmed. The same couldn't be said for Ribbit's bottom, which he was sure would be sporting a giant bruise come tomorrow—if he made it to tomorrow.

Ribbit shot up and quickly shoved Zippy behind him, so that he could protect her. As he stood to face the giant bird, he was surprised to see familiar spotted brown feathers.

"Ollie!" Ribbit clutched his chest. "You scared the daylights out of me!"

"I do apologize, Ribbit. I didn't mean to alarm you, or anyone for that matter." He glanced around at the hundreds of frog eyes peering at him through the clear glass and did his best to give an "I'm sorry and I mean you no harm" smile. They weren't buying it.

"Whew! Boy, am I glad to see you! I thought I was a goner!" Ribbit exhaled as he looked up into the amber eyes of his dear friend. Zippy still hid behind Ribbit, in shock of the giant bird before her.

"Lucky thing since you so strangely offered yourself up, standing out here alone rather than following your friends to safety," Ollie winked. "Nevertheless, I have come here to give you something." He lifted up his talons to reveal a book; but it wasn't just any old book, it was *Sparrow's Journey Home*.

Ribbit felt as if he was on the top of the world! He couldn't contain a squeal of delight as he ran up to hug his dear friend. "Thank you! Thank you! Thank you!"

"You're very welcome, Ribbit," Ollie said warmly.

"Where did you find it?" he asked as he grabbed the book and stared at it as if he had never seen it before.

"Momma found it on the floor in the library. She figured it must have fallen out when you gathered your belongings this morning. Since I knew it must be of great importance to you, I decided to come back right away. I do hope I didn't cause too much trouble being here."

"Not at all! I couldn't be happier to see you!" Ribbit hopped excitedly.

"One more thing, before I get going." Ollie presented Ribbit with a small, ornate brass key. "It's a key to the Enchanted Meadow. Our little way of letting you know that our door is always open."

"Wow!" Ribbit smiled as he took hold of the key. "I will treasure it forever, Ollie. Thanks." He gripped the key tightly to his chest. He always knew that he would return home from his great conquest with treasure.

"I do hope that you will use it, Ribbit. Now, I must be off before I give any of your neighbors a heart attack." Ollie gave a little chuckle. "Take care of yourself, Ribbit." And with that, Ollie spread his giant wings and took off into the sky, leaving only a gust of autumn leaves in his wake.

"Good-bye, Ollie!" Ribbit called out, but the great owl was already gone.

Slowly, the frogs began to stagger out of the shops, bewildered as if their own eyes had deceived them. There was no doubting that Ribbit's fantastic tale was true, and after Ollie's guest appearance, even Squiggy and Kilroy couldn't deny that now.

Through the crowds of frogs streaming into Main Street, Phinn and Croak suddenly appeared.

"Hey, what happened? We were in Backwater Café ordering a mosquito milkshake when all of a sudden the whole town came piling in going on about some bird. What happened?" Phinn's glasses were crooked and he was covered in mosquito milkshake, which had undoubtedly been spilled during all of the commotion.

"It was Ollie," Ribbit smiled.

"No way!" Croak looked up into the empty, blue sky above.

"Ah, man! You mean we missed him?" Phinn grunted crossly, kicking up dirt.

"Yeah, but he returned my book and he left us this." Ribbit held out the key and both of their eyes lit up.

"Is that what I think it is?" Phinn asked, a smile dancing across his face.

"Absolutely." Ribbit handed it over to Phinn.

"What? What is it?" Croak asked.

"A key to the Enchanted Meadow, algae brain," Phinn teased as he inspected the key, running his fingers along its every curve.

"Cool." Croak shrugged, seemingly not feeling as honored or excited as Ribbit and Phinn.

"Yes, Croak. It's very cool," Ribbit giggled. "Now let's get this celebration going again. Hit it, maestro!" Ribbit pointed at the band, and the sounds of banjos and drums filled the air with their sweet music, bringing the festival back to life.

The Comforts of Home

After hours of dancing, celebrating, and lots of fly eating, the festivities began to die down and the McFly family headed home.

Ribbit delighted in taking part in their usual nighttime routine. He eagerly helped Zippy into her pajamas before changing into his own. They felt so soft and comforting on his skin. As he headed into the hallway, he could hear the teakettle whistling in the kitchen, signifying that tea was ready. Ribbit let out a giggle as he raced to the living room to join his family for a cup of hot tea and a good book.

"Alright, kiddo. What'll it be tonight?" Ribbit's father asked as he poked at the fire, its flames thriving and the wood crackling.

The choice was a no-brainer for Ribbit! He knew exactly what he wanted to read: *Sparrow's Journey Home*. Ever since Shelly had given him the book, he had imagined what it would sound like to have his father read it aloud to him, the words coming to life in a way only his father could make happen. He handed the book to his father and snuggled in between his parents, soaking in the moment and feeling the warmth and comfort of home.

When the story was over it was time to go to bed. Zippy insisted on sleeping in Ribbit's room with him since it was his first night home, even if it meant that she had to sleep on the floor. Of course, Ribbit agreed and his parents made up a bed out of extra blankets for Zippy. Then they tucked her in and gave her a kiss before sitting on the end of Ribbit's bed.

"It's good to have you home, kiddo," his father said, his voice brimming with love.

"We're just so glad you're back, Ribbykins," his mother added, giving him a big, wet kiss on his cheek. He usually would wipe off his mother's slobbery kisses, but since he had missed her so much, he let this one stay. "We're very proud of you, but don't you ever think of pulling a stunt like that again!" She giggled, a tear in her eye.

"You must be exhausted, little fella. Get to sleep. But first," his father paused for a moment. "Ribbit, I love you more than there are words in a story."

"And I love you more than there are flies in your belly," his mother said as she gave him a tickle.

As Ribbit stared up at his parents, he felt as if his heart was going to explode like a warm, gooey water balloon. While he would never trade his adventure for anything, nothing compared to being home with the frogs who loved him most.

They kissed him gently on the head and uncovered his firefly nightlight, lighting up the room with its familiar glow, before creeping out and closing the door behind them.

Snuggled under his fluffy comforter, he breathed in deeply, his head sinking into his downy pillow. The full moon cast golden shadows on his bedroom walls as his curtains fluttered softly in the evening breeze. Zippy's soft breathing came from the floor. He could also hear the muffled sounds of his mom humming as she and his father cleaned up the kitchen before going to bed. The embers in the stone fireplace crackled and popped occasionally and the familiar old clock ticked rhythmically. All was well with the world.

Feeling very content, and very grown up, Ribbit felt his eyes grow weary as he drifted off to sleep, dreaming of his next great adventure.

About the Author

Kylie O'Brien Hall is an Elementary School Teacher in the San Francisco Bay Area. During her first year of teaching, she decided that her students needed a classroom pet, but preferably a pet that wouldn't leave her any "special surprises" to clean up. Her solution: a loveable stuffed animal named Ribbit the Frog. From the very first day, Ribbit magically came to life. The students delighted in hearing about his imaginary adventures, which inspired Kylie to put them in writing. Now children everywhere can enjoy reading about Ribbit's adventures in an imaginary world where animals can talk and even the least-likely of frogs can be a hero.

The adventures continue!

Look for the second book of
The Grand Adventures of Ribbit the Frog Series:
The Destruction of the Enchanted Meadow.

Visit Kylie and Ribbit online at: **www.kylieobrienhall.com**

Made in the USA
Charleston, SC
23 May 2012